A gorgeous couple

Dear **D**iary:

I'm a wreck, an absolute wreck. I finally asked my brother Adam to show me how to dance.

"Lizzie!" Adam shouted. "Take your arm from around my neck! You're choking me! . . . You're terrible, Lizzie!"

I went up to my room and threw myself on the bed. I am hopeless. If they do play slow dances, and any boy happens to ask me to dance, I will cripple him. No doubt.

I went over to my closet and opened the door. That gave me an idea. I put on my radio and flipped the dial until I found a slow tune. Then I grabbed hold of the closet doorknob and danced back and forth. It all worked wonderfully.

If I could just take the door to the dance with me, I'd be fine.

Suddenly I knew someone was watching me. Gram was standing in my room, and she had a hand covering her mouth, but her eyes told me she was laughing.

"Don't laugh," I warned her.

"Who's laughing?" she asked. "You and the door make a gorgeous couple."

Dear Diary

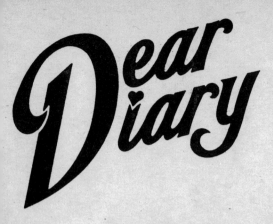

THE DANCE

Carrie Randall

AN
APPLE
PAPERBACK

SCHOLASTIC INC.
New York Toronto London Auckland Sydney

ISBN 0-590-42478-5

12 11 10 9 8 7 6 5 4 3   0 1 2 3 4 5/9

Printed in the U.S.A.

First Scholastic printing, February 1990

KEEP OUT!!
(This means you!)

This diary is the property
of
Elizabeth
Jane
Miletti

ALL TRESPASSERS WILL BE
PROSECUTED!

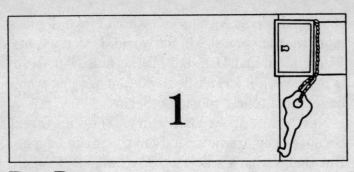

Dear **D**iary:

You're a new diary, but I guess you know that. Gram gave you to me for Christmas, and I have to get used to you. My old diary, the one I wrote in last year, was so familiar to me, but you certainly are much more beautiful . . . and more expensive.

Do I have to tell you all about me? Or do old diaries and new diaries meet in some wonderful diaryland and exchange information? I guess not. SOO, to get it all over with quickly: I'm Lizzie Miletti, eleven years old. I'm in sixth grade and my best friend is Nancy Underpeace and my worst friend (I guess that would make her my enemy) is stuck-up Samantha Howard. My father works for Roth Frozen Food Company and is always forcing new products (mostly awful things) on us. My mother used to be a nurse but gave it up when all us kids started arriving. I have two brothers: Adam, thirteen; Josh, sixteen; and two sisters: Darcy, eight; and Rose, four. And then there is

Gram, who lives with us and whom I love, I guess more than anyone else in the world. Is that wrong? I love Mom and Dad and all the kids, but Gram is my favorite. I can't lie to you, or we just won't have much to say to each other.

New years are a little scary. They are great because they are new, and anything can happen. But that's what's scary . . . anything can happen. Last year I know. And even though it wasn't all good, at least it's not a mystery. I mean, I know that Nancy and I had a terrible fight and didn't talk for days. *She* didn't talk to me; *I* was willing. But we made up. And Gram started dating Mr. Bagnold, and I was worried that maybe they would get married and Gram would move out. But that obviously isn't going to happen, because Gram is still here and seems perfectly happy. She still dates . . . what a dumb word for an older woman, date — it sounds so teenagey . . . but that's what they're doing. Mr. Bagnold is nice. I guess I like him, as long as he knows his place, which is *not* as Gram's husband.

So here I am beginning a new year, ready or not.

Everyone in school, in my grade that is, but *everyone* is talking about The Dance. It is *The* Dance, like the most important thing in the world. It isn't even going to take place until April, but the kids are carrying on as if it were tomorrow.

2

And all it is going to be is a dumb sixth-grade dance in the dumb gym, but it *is* a first. The first sixth-grade dance. Nancy and I talked about it on the way home from school today.

"I'm not going," Nancy said, kicking a stone in front of her as far as she could.

"What do you mean you're not going?" I asked her. "How do you know? It's months and months away."

"I know!" Nancy said in her Nancy way: firm and stubborn. "Dances just aren't my thing."

I laughed . . . in a not very nice way. I think a novelist would call it scornful. "You've never even *been* to a dance, so how do you know it's not your thing? That is a very prejudiced thing to say."

Then Nancy laughed in that scornful way. "Prejudiced? That's something you say about people who don't like other people. It isn't used to refer to dances."

She looked so self-satisfied, I could have swatted her. But I didn't say anything more. I didn't want to make fun of how she uses words. Nancy is dyslexic . . . that means she sees words in some kind of funny way, which makes it hard for her to read. I, her very best friend, didn't even know it until a few months ago. She somehow managed to keep it a secret, probably because she can memorize like crazy. Now she's getting help with her problem and is getting better.

Getting back to the subject of the dance, I said to Nancy, "You have to keep an open mind. You can't decide months ahead that you're not going to the social high of the sixth grade."

"I can decide any time I want," Nancy said. "And I've decided . . . I'm not going. I'm not ready for dances. Maybe I'll never be."

"That's what I mean," I persisted. "Maybe you'll mature in the next few months and be dying to go."

Nancy stopped walking and glared at me. "In other words, you think I'm immature now."

I knew I was in trouble because that is *just* what I think. We've even talked about it. Nancy wants to stay a kid forever, and I want to grow and grow and grow. I want to be sophisticated. "You've said it yourself, Nancy. You don't want to be a teenager. You want to stay a little girl."

Nancy narrowed her lips and put her hands on her hips. "*You*, Elizabeth Miletti, are *not* a teenager. You are eleven years old. That means you won't be a teenager for another *two* years. So stop acting so smart. Or else go be best friends with Samantha Howard. You think she's so cool anyway."

We had reached my house, and Nancy didn't even stop for a second. She just kept walking. "Don't you want to come in?" I asked.

"Not today," Nancy said and walked off.

I sighed. We had done it again . . . had a fight. It happened so often. It's hard being a best friend. And Nancy was right, I do think Samantha Howard is cool . . . and beautiful . . . and the best-dressed girl in the sixth grade . . . and the meanest. She made it clear to me months ago that the only reason she bothered to say boo to me was because of Adam. And Adam doesn't know she's alive.

That's another reason Nancy and I had fought. She knew when Samantha started trying to be my friend that Samantha had an ulterior motive. And she had been right, the ulterior motive being Adam. That had been tough, accepting the fact that Samantha didn't care beans for me. In fact she probably thought I was a nerd.

Sometimes I feel like a nerd, especially when I look in the mirror. I wish I were tall, like Nancy, instead of short like me. I wish I didn't have frizzy, wild hair. I wish I had long, straight, blonde hair, like Nancy. But other times I feel good about me, like I'm really special.

The house was its usual noisy self when I walked in the door. Rose and Darcy were in the kitchen with Mom, who was trying to incorporate Dad's latest food delight, multi-colored string beans, into something for dinner. Baby Rose (why do we still call her "Baby"?) was overjoyed by them and was eating them frozen. Darcy had more sense. "These are disgusting," she said.

My mother nodded. "I know, but try humoring your father a little . . . don't tell him." She looked up at me and smiled. "How did your day go?"

"Fine," I said. I have to admit I haven't told Mom or Dad about the dance. Mainly because I know that Dad will be freaked out by the idea of his "little" girl, me, going to a dance. And Mom? I don't know what she'll say. So I thought I'd just wait and drop it into the conversation sometime when everyone is in a good mood and listening to what I have to say, which might be never.

I patted Rose on the head as she munched on a red string bean.

"Is Gram home?"

Gram sells real estate, so she's out of the house a lot. I think Mom is jealous. I mean, I think she'd like to be out of the house a lot, too, but when you have five kids, it's hard not to be home a lot. Although I think that Mom might go back to nursing soon, at least part-time. I can tell she is getting restless and a little bored trying to think up new ways to use Dad's gross new products.

"She's upstairs," Mom said. "If you're going up, take that pile of towels with you."

I ran up to Gram's little apartment and was about to knock on her door. That is one thing Gram has taught me, that everyone is entitled to privacy, and everyone should knock on everyone's door before going into a room. I was just about to — really, I had my knuckles all ready to knock — when I heard this laugh. It was Gram's laugh, but not Gram's. It had a different sound, soft and low and very warm. Gram's laugh is generally loud and bubbly.

Then I heard her say, "What time are you picking me up, Ralph?"

I was suddenly shocked — at myself. I was eavesdropping. It wasn't the first time I had done that, I have to admit it. But it was the first time I had ever done that to my grandmother. But sometimes you just have to eavesdrop to find out what is going on in your own life. Ralph is Mr. Bagnold. And the way Gram was talking to Mr. Bagnold sounded to me like the way Samantha Howard talks to a boy she likes.

Well, I know Gram likes Mr. Bagnold, but that laugh made me wonder, how *much* does she like him? Well, no, it wasn't how much, it was *how*. Before I could think further, I knocked on the door.

"Come in," Gram called out.

She was sitting in a chair filing her nails, and when she looked up and saw me she smiled that grandma smile. "Hi, sweetie."

I had come to talk to her about the dance, but

it seemed unimportant at that minute. "I hope I wasn't interrupting you. I heard you on the phone just before I knocked." That was getting right to the point, I thought.

"Oh, yes. That was Ralph . . . Mr. Bagnold. He's coming by, and we're going out to dinner."

"Oh," I said.

Gram looked at me carefully. "Lizzie, we're friends. Good friends . . . Friends go out to dinner together."

I felt a feeling of relief that started at my toes and went up to my eyebrows. All they are is friends. That's okay. That's fine.

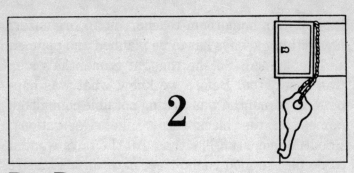

2

Dear **D**iary:

I can't believe it, but Samantha actually suggested in homeroom this morning that we form committees to work on the dance. You know, *The* Dance. Even though it's months until the big event takes place, Samantha is probably already figuring out what she's going to wear. Of course, as soon as the words were out of her mouth, Candace Quinn and Jessica Arnold, Samantha's best friends, started oohing and aahing and saying, "What a *wonderful* idea." They would think it was a wonderful idea if Samantha suggested they jump out the window. You know, maybe that *is* a good idea. You see how mean and angry Samantha makes me?

Anyway, I heard Nancy gagging in her seat behind me, and a lot of the other kids in the class were turned off by the idea, too. The boys started hooting and punching each other in the arms, and shouting "You wanna dance with me, Sammy?" and the girls just looked a little nervous. But Ms.

Basley, our homeroom teacher, is an organizer. Everything always has to be planned and planned and replanned. So she thought Samantha's idea was great, too. Before we knew what was happening, Samantha was writing possible committee names on the blackboard. Like, Decorations, Food, Music, stuff like that. All the boys wanted to be on the food committee, naturally. I wasn't going to volunteer for anything, since I haven't even told my parents about this dance, but Ms. Basley insisted I pick something, so I figured decorations was the easiest. I mean, what do you have to know about decorations? It seems to me that any jerk can do that.

Nancy absolutely refused to be on *any* committee, even though I turned around, gave her my most annoyed look, and whispered to her, "Grow up!" She even stood up, cleared her throat, and said, loud, too, "I'm not coming to this dance. I think the whole idea stinks."

Ms. Basley objected to the word "stinks," and then there were twenty kids, all yelling, "She's right, it stinks," or "No, it doesn't stink," or "Sit down, Nancy."

When we left school, Ericka Powell and Nancy and I walked home together. Ericka is a neat girl. She used to live in Alaska. I think the cold weather sort of made her very laid back, because she always seems so calm and sane. She said to Nancy, "You didn't really mean it that you weren't going to the dance, did you?"

Nancy pouted in her typical Nancy way. "Of course I meant it. It's a dumb idea, and I don't want to dance with any dumb boy."

I huffed, "What makes you even think any dumb boy is going to ask us to dance? With Samantha there, looking gorgeous and knowing all the new dances, and Jessica and Candace hanging around her, looking equally gorgeous, we'll probably fade into the woodwork."

Nancy stopped walking and laughed. "*That* sure makes me want to go. Now we're all going to be wallflowers."

Ericka looked really thoughtful. "Why do we have to wait for a boy to ask *us* to dance? Why can't *we* ask *them*?"

"It's my first dance, Ericka," I said, "and I can't see myself asking a boy to dance."

"Ericka is right," Nancy said, with a superior tone. "If you want to go to the dance in the first place, you should also want to ask a boy to dance. That makes sense to me."

We had reached my house, and I glared at Nancy. "You don't know anything about dances. So how would you know what makes sense? You're not even brave enough to go." With that, I turned around and ran into my house.

11

You know, this dance is going to make real problems for Nancy and me. As if we didn't have enough of them.

Well, Diary, at dinner I finally brought up the whole subject of this dance. I knew I had to do it sooner or later. I waited for a quiet moment, or at least a quieter moment, and I just said, "The sixth grade is going to have a dance in a couple of months."

Gram looked up from the chicken we were eating and said, "That's nice. Your first real dance, right?"

I nodded and tried to peek at my father's face without looking right at him. My dad is funny. He's really good about a lot of things with us kids. Like, we get good allowances, and he doesn't lecture us about being responsible citizens, and he doesn't scream if we don't always do so great in school. BUT I know he doesn't really see that I'm growing up. I have to admit, for my dad it's okay if Adam and Josh mature, but not me. I guess there's a certain amount of male chauvinism in him.

I was ready. "You mean a dance with boys?" he asked.

Mom laughed. "Well, there *are* boys in her class, Bob. It's a class dance, from what Lizzie says."

Dad pushed his plate away from him and shook his head. "I don't know. Isn't Elizabeth a little young for this kind of thing?"

I knew as soon as he said "Elizabeth" I was in trouble. That's what he calls me when he's ready for a serious talk.

"Dad," I said. "It's a dance in the school gym, at four-thirty in the afternoon on a Friday, with teachers there and everything. It's no big deal."

"It's a big deal to me," Dad said.

"It's just a symbol to you," Adam said firmly.

I wasn't sure whether that meant Adam was on my side or not, so I waited to see where this was all going.

"Okay, Dr. Freud," Dad said. "A symbol of what?"

"That Lizzie is growing up. Dancing with boys and stuff. She'll be dating soon and then going to college and getting a job, maybe in New York, and maybe getting married and having kids."

"Gee, thanks, Adam," I said, looking at my father's eyes getting wider and wider. "You're really a big help."

"I think it's great," Darcy said.

"Me, too," Rose piped up. "I want to go to the dance, too."

Josh stood up and started clearing the table. "Well, I personally think she's not ready. Not mature enough to know how to handle herself at a

13

dance. She's too young. And I know boys that age can be *pretty* rowdy."

"You are a stuffed shirt, Josh," I spit out at him. "You always were and always will be. And anyway, who asked you?"

Mom clapped her hands loudly. "Okay, kids, stop the bickering. Josh, Lizzie is right, it's none of your business. In fact, it's none of any of your business. This is something for your father and me to decide."

"Can I have a say in this?" Gram asked, winking at me.

"We already know what your say is, Mother," my mom said. "Okay, everyone can leave the table and let Bob and me talk about this."

"It's my life," I said, and I could feel tears coming into my eyes. As you know, Diary, I'm a crier. Whenever things get tough, I cry. I hate it, but I do. "I want to stay, too."

"Okay," Dad said. "You're right. You stay. But no tears, Lizzie. You have to be a grown-up."

I knew I had him then . . . and so did my mother. I could see a little smile around her mouth. "If I have to be a grown-up about crying, then why can't I be a grown-up about dances? That's fair, isn't it?"

"We aren't talking about fair," Dad said. "We're talking about my little girl going to a dance . . . with boys."

14

"Dad, you are . . . are . . . medieval."

Mom burst out laughing. "Bob, you sound just like my father did when I wanted to go to my first dance. Exactly. Bob, it's a *school* dance. In the gym. At four-thirty in the afternoon. Be reasonable."

Dad looked at me. "All right. But the only reason Lizzie is going is because I don't want to be compared to your father, Lynn. He was a curmudgeon."

"What's a curmudgeon?" I asked.

"Look it up in the dictionary," Dad said. "*Before* you go to the dance."

I ran around the table to him and put my arms around him. "Thanks," I said, and kissed his cheek.

I looked up *curmudgeon* in the dictionary, and it said, "An irascible, churlish fellow." That wasn't much help. So I looked up *churlish*. The first thing it said was, "Of a churl or churls." Why do they do that? If I knew what "of a churl" meant, I wouldn't have been looking up churlish. But then it also said "rude." That I understood. Then I looked up *irascible*, and that said, "Easily provoked to anger." My grandfather, who died before I was born, doesn't sound like he was so hot. But I guess if Gram loved him, being churlish once in a while can't be so awful.

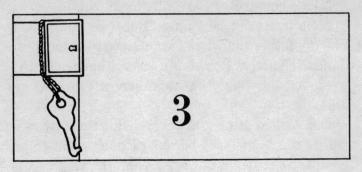

3

Dear **D**iary:

Last night after I'd been asleep for a while, I woke up and felt really cold. I had opened my window before I went to sleep, so I got up to close it. While I was standing at the window, I looked out onto the street. Mr. Bagnold had just driven up to the house, bringing Gram home from a date. He got out of the car and ran around to the other side to open the door for Gram. He does that all the time. Well, when she got out, he put his arms around her and kissed her. I mean *really* kissed her. Not a peck on the cheek; not a *quick* kiss on her mouth. He kissed her a *long* time. And she put her hands up on his shoulders and held onto him.

I just stared at them and could hardly breathe. Then I heard her say, "Goodnight, Ralph, dear."

Dear. That's what she said. When I heard her coming up the stairs, I quickly turned off my little bed light. Sometimes, if Gram sees a light under my door, she comes into my room to talk. But I just couldn't talk to her last night. I couldn't.

I got back into bed and carefully went over everything I had seen and heard. I was looking for something that would reassure me. But kissing and hugging and saying dear is not reassuring, no matter what. I may not have much experience with boys myself . . . no, change that, *any* experience with boys myself, but I do watch TV and go to the movies, and I know romance when I see it. And Mr. Bagnold and Gram were definitely romantic.

I felt so alone and confused and scared that I got up and found Turtles — that's a stuffed animal that goes back practically to babyhood. Turtles is a turtle, obviously. I clutched Turtles to me and just lay there with the tears dripping onto my pillow. If Mr. Bagnold and Gram were romantic, what did that mean?

I couldn't wait to talk to Nancy about it at lunchtime today. I was so upset that I even bought the day's special in the cafeteria. *No one*, but no one, in his or her right mind ever buys the special. It is usually impossible to tell what it is, and the nutritionist doesn't help any in clearing up the mystery because she always names it something like Tuesday Delight or Creative Casserole. Anyway, when I sat down next to Nancy at our table, she looked at my lunch and said, "You bought the special? What's wrong?"

I gazed at the gray mess and said, "I wasn't thinking. Anyway, *you* don't have to eat it."

Nancy nodded. "But I have to look at it."

She took a napkin and just covered the thing up. "Nancy," I began, "Gram and Mr. Bagnold were kissing last night."

Nancy shrugged. "Well, you said they were friends. Friends kiss."

"No," I said, "this was not friends kissing. This was kissing kissing."

"Really?" Nancy said, totally interested. "Your Gram is really something. I read this article called 'Love after Fifty' in a magazine my mom has. You know, my reading teacher said I should read anything that interests me and not feel it has to be important, or I have to learn anything from it. She just wants me to read."

"That makes sense," I said. "So what about this article, and why should love after fifty interest you?"

"My mom is going to be fifty someday, and I just thought I should be prepared."

I don't know if I mentioned that Nancy's mom and dad are divorced, and they both date sometimes.

"So what did the article say?" I asked, taking half of Nancy's tuna sandwich.

"It says you are never too old to fall in love, and it's right and good and all nice things. So your Gram is lucky." Nancy grabbed back the tuna half I had taken.

I glared at Nancy. "Would you think it was so lucky if your mother fell in love and got married, or your dad?"

Nancy was thoughtful. "My dad . . . it wouldn't matter that much. I only go there some weekends and then, as you know, he's so busy amusing me, it's hard to concentrate."

Diary, you know how Nancy's father has this nonstop schedule for them when Nancy goes to visit. But he *is* getting better.

"Okay, so what about your mom?" I asked.

"That would be tough. I mean, the guy would move in and everything. But she's my mom. A grandmother is different. What would be so awful if Mr. Bagnold moved in?" Nancy asked me.

I wanted to punch her. Nancy can be so thick. "Nancy," I said, speaking slowly, as if she were two years old. "No man would marry Gram and move into our house, into Gram's tiny apartment, what with five kids and my mom and dad. If Gram got married she would move *out*. Forever." Tears came to my eyes, and I tried to brush them away quickly, but Nancy saw them.

She reached over and took my hand. "I'm sorry," she whispered.

Nancy can be soooo sweet sometimes.

When I got home from school Mom was in the kitchen, sitting at the table. She had a list in front of her, her co-op list, and she was holding a pencil in her hand . . . but she was just sitting and staring into space. She looked at me when I came in, but she didn't say anything. She looked so funny that she scared me.

"Are you sick or something?" I asked her.

Now she looked at me. "Oh, hi, Lizzie. What did you say?"

"I asked if you were sick. You look so weird."

"Lizzie, sit down."

I started to sit, when she waved a hand at me. "No, don't sit. I think you should go up to your grandmother. She's in her apartment. I think she wants to talk to you."

"Is *she* sick?" I asked.

My mom shook her head. "No, she's fine. Just go up."

As I turned to leave the room, I saw tears in my mother's eyes . . . and my mom never cries, but never. At least not in front of us kids. So I ran upstairs . . . but I knew. I really did.

Gram was sitting in a chair in her living room.

Like my mom, she was just sitting, too. When I came in, she at least looked at me and smiled.

"Mom said you had something to tell me," I said to her.

"Sit down, Lizzie." I wished everyone would stop telling me to sit down, and talk to me.

Gram leaned forward and took my hands. "Lizzie, dear, Mr. Bagnold and I are going to get married." She waited for me to take all that in, and then she said. "I am very happy. At least I was until I told your mother, but she isn't very happy about it at all and that makes me not so happy about it, too."

I tried to look into Gram's eyes. I tried to tell her if she was happy I was, too, but nothing came out of my mouth.

"I love Ralph a lot," Gram said, "and he loves me . . . and we want to be together."

"You said you were just friends." I know I sounded as if I was accusing her of lying or something.

"No, I didn't say 'just friends,' I said we were friends . . . and we are. But we also care about each other in more, or different, ways than friends do. We want to be married. Can you understand that, Lizzie?"

I swallowed hard. "You won't live here anymore, will you?"

21

"No, I won't. But I won't be far away. Ralph has a house near here. You know that. We'll be close by."

I told you, Diary, I am a crier. Well, I started to cry. I thought Gram would come over and put her arms around me. But she just sat in her chair and looked out the nearby window.

"I didn't think I was going to cause such an uproar. First your mother, and now you. You know, Lizzie, I am not committing a federal crime. I am just getting married."

I couldn't help it, but in between sobs I said, "You love him more than you do me."

Then she did what I wanted her to do all along; she took me into her arms and hugged me tight. "Oh, no, Lizzie, not more at all . . . just in a different way. I will always love you. Lizzie, he's a nice man. I thought you liked him."

Actually, Ralph isn't bad. I kind of think his being shaped like a cookie jar is sort of cute. And the way he tries to hide his bald spot by combing what little hair he has over it, makes me want to giggle. He is always nice to me, and I know he wants me to like him. But his marrying Gram and taking her away makes me hate him.

"Gram, I thought you and I would never change, that we'd always be in the same house."

Gram smiled, actually smiled, at a time like that. "Don't you intend to go away to college? Or have your own apartment someday? Or get married someday?" she asked.

"Well, of course. It's just that I thought *you'd* always be here and now . . . and now. . . ."

I couldn't say another word. I felt so lonely, and I hurt so, I just ran out of Gram's apartment and down the stairs into my room.

Dear Diary, I am so miserable. I can't believe my very own gram is going to leave me. I know I should be a good person and feel happy for her, but how can I feel happy about someone when she is feeling happy because she's leaving me? It's a very hard thing to do.

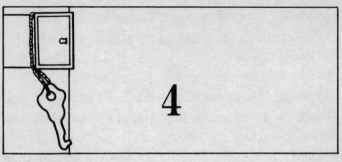

4

Dear **D**iary:

The house has been like a funeral parlor, or some kind of divided place, since Gram told us she was getting married. Everyone is either walking around looking like they are going to die or throw up, or they are glaring at each other. The Milettis have had fights, we've disagreed, we've not spoken to each other, but never like this. In fact, things got so bad that Dad called a meeting in the den a couple of nights ago.

When we were all together, except for Gram — she wasn't asked to come, and you'll soon see why — Dad started talking. "I think this family has some serious thinking and some serious talking to do. Now, Gram has announced that she is getting married."

At that point, Baby Rose burst into tears . . . and believe me, Rose is a *loud* crier. "Gramma is going," she sobbed. "Mean Mr. Bagnold. I hate him."

I couldn't have agreed more, but before I could

say anything, Dad looked at Rose and said loudly and firmly, "Rose, keep quiet and stop your crying. I'm talking."

I have never, but never, heard Dad talk to Rose like that. She is his delight . . . the baby . . . his angel. Rose was horrified, but she shut up, and Dad went on. "We should all be happy for Gram. She has been a widow for twelve years, and for a good part of those years she has devoted herself to this family. Now, finally, and about time, she is going to have a new life of her own with a very nice man."

"Right," Darcy said. "Good for Gram. And Ralph is a sweetie."

Dad smiled at Darcy. "Well, there is one intelligent, unselfish person in this family."

Sweetie? How could Darcy ever call Ralph Bagnold a sweetie? I thought.

"Wait a minute," Adam said. "I'm glad she's getting married, too. I'm just as intelligent as Darcy any day . . . not that that says much."

Darcy got up and was about to walk over to Adam and punch him in the arm, when Dad grabbed her. "Sit," he said. Darcy sat.

Josh carefully smoothed back his already smooth hair . . . Josh is into smooth hair right now. He thinks it's cool. "Well, I think she's too old to get married. That's for young people, not the elderly."

"Gram is *not* elderly," Darcy shouted. "And you are, like Lizzie says, a stuffed shirt."

Josh *is* a stuffed shirt, and I agree Gram is not elderly, but at least Josh was on my side this time.

Dad looked at my mother and said gently, "Well, Lynn, we haven't heard anything from you."

My mother just looked down at her hands, where she was twisting a handkerchief. Then she said, so softly that I almost couldn't hear her, "I'll just miss her so. She's been here so long . . . and we hardly know Ralph."

"Well, we'll all miss her," Dad said. "But we aren't the ones who have to know and love Ralph, Gram is."

"I just think she should wait," Mom said. "Give us a chance to talk more about this, to get used to it. I never thought this would happen." Mom put her handkerchief up and dried her eyes.

I reached for a Kleenex in my jeans' pocket and dried my eyes, too. It was hard, because the tissue had bits of lint and a peanut stuck to it, and some ink on it. I looked at my mother and I must admit I thought it was funny that *she* was crying. After all, she is a grown-up. I'm just a kid. I didn't think grown-ups cried when their parents went away.

"Okay," Dad said. "I want everyone here to stop acting as if the world were ending, and start thinking a little about Gram. Class dismissed."

26

I *was* thinking about Gram. I was thinking that she wasn't going to be around anymore.

Just as we were all leaving the den, Gram appeared. She looked wonderful, smiling, happy, full of energy. She put her arm around my mom's shoulders and said, "Oh, Ralph just called. He wants to take us all out to dinner tomorrow night, so we can make plans for the wedding. Nothing fancy, of course — dinner that is — since there is such a mob of us. But we are eager to talk about what kind of a wedding — where, who, that kind of thing."

"Well," Dad said, sounding sooo cheery. "That's very generous of Ralph. We'd all be *happy* to go. Right, Lynn?"

Mom just looked at Gram and ran out of the room. I could see the expression on Gram's face change. The happy look left, and there was one of worry and confusion that took its place. But she couldn't think she could just announce she was going to get married and not have us all upset, could she? Or at least, most of us upset.

The next day as I sat in history class, I just tried to think about what it would be like when we all went out with Ralph that night. As you know, history is not my best subject, so to be worried about something else in history, besides history, is death. I could hear Mr. Burrows droning on about something or other, but I couldn't have said what.

Suddenly I heard his voice saying, "Elizabeth. Elizabeth Miletti, are you here? And if not, where are you?"

Nancy, who sits behind me, poked me in the shoulder, hard, and I jumped. The class all burst out laughing when they saw me practically leap out of my seat. "I'm sorry, Mr. Burrows, I . . . I guess I wasn't listening. What was the question?"

"The question, Elizabeth, is are you again going to put us all through the big mystery of whether you are going to pass the next test? We seem to wonder regularly."

He was right, of course. I am always almost failing history. If it weren't for Nancy, dyslexia and all, I would have failed a million times.

"Okay, Mr. Burrows, you have my total attention now."

"Wonders will never cease, Elizabeth. Okay, the question was, 'What do you think this country would be like if the Revolution had never taken place?' "

I was speechless. Then I finally said, "To tell you the truth, Mr. Burrows, I never really thought about that."

"Fine, Elizabeth. Think about it now. These questions are put to you kids to *make* you think about things you have never bothered with before."

"Can I think about it tonight and let you know tomorrow?" I asked eagerly.

Mr. Burrows sighed . . . loudly. "Okay, Elizabeth, you do that. Nancy, what do you think?"

Poor Nancy, I thought, but Nancy, quick as anything, said, "Well, we might still be a colony, and we might never have added all the states besides the original thirteen colonies."

I turned around and stared at Nancy with awe. She may not read so well, but she sure can think.

"Very good, Nancy. Very good indeed," Mr. Burrows said.

When we met to walk home, Nancy said with annoyance, "Lizzie, you have to pay attention in history. I can't spend my whole life getting you a passing grade. I have my own troubles."

"I know, I know. And I have mine, too. Gram is getting married and moving into Mr. Bagnold's house, and it's probably going to be soon because we are all meeting tonight to discuss the wedding." I stopped to catch my breath.

"How romantic!" Nancy cooed. I could have swatted her.

"Romantic!" I shouted. "Some friend you are! My gram is moving away, and all you can say is it's romantic. Sometimes I think you are heartless, Nancy Underpeace."

Nancy stopped walking and glared at me. "Listen, Lizzie, my own *father* has moved out of *my* house. So a *grandmother* doesn't seem so dreadful to me. Think about that."

She was right, of course. And I *had* forgotten that her father was gone, but just because Nancy's father left doesn't make it any easier that my grandmother is going. Diary, why do people always think that if you have some problem that is less than someone else's, it makes yours not so important or crucial? I just don't understand that. It would be like if I had broken my leg and someone else had broken both a leg and an arm, it would make *my* leg hurt less. You know what I mean?

Well, we all went out together for dinner, and it was a zoo. A real zoo. I guess when nine people all eat together, you can figure it's going to be a mob scene. We went to a hamburger place, but one that has big tables and where a waitress comes and serves you. First it was a big deal until everyone decided what they wanted to eat. Then when the waitress came to take our orders, Rose and Josh kept changing their minds. My dad was trying to stick to a diet (he is a little chunky), and so was Ralph; Mom is allergic to certain foods; Darcy wanted to try anything new on the menu;

Gram was nervous and wasn't too hungry, and neither was I. I just wanted to get the whole thing over with.

Dad tried to be jovial. In fact he was so ho-ho that he made Santa Claus seem depressed. He kept looking at Mom, and once I even saw him poke her in the arm to remind her to smile. It seems to me poking isn't the best way to get someone to smile.

Finally Ralph said, almost as jovially as Dad, "Well, I guess it's time for Betty and me to talk about our wedding plans."

Gram smiled and said, "That's what we're here for."

"Okay, Betty, what do you want?" Dad said. "It's your wedding, and we'll do whatever it is that will please you and Ralph."

At that moment, Rose let out a wail and got under the table. I knew how she felt, and if I weren't eleven years old I would have joined her. Everyone then tried to get Rose to come out and eat her dinner, but Rose can be really stubborn, and she refused.

Dad said very firmly, "If that's what she wants, let her stay there."

Mom kept peering under the table, and she said to my father, "That's cruel, Bob. The baby is just upset."

"Lynn," he said, "Rose is four years old. She is

not a baby, and let's stop calling her that."

That produced another wail from Rose, and Mom glared at my father. Darcy said, "It's about time someone realized that. After all, she is only four years younger than I am, and nobody pampers me the way they do her."

Gram sighed. "Look, this is not a family problem-solving meeting. This is to talk about my wedding. Now, Ralph and I decided we would like to be married at home. If that's all right with you, Lynn. Just a few people in my own home. All of us, Ralph's children, and some friends."

My mother twisted a strand of hair around her finger. She does that, just like a kid, when she's upset. "Well, the house is a little small for a lot of people, Mother. . . ."

My dad put his arm around Mom's shoulders and said, "Lynn, that isn't a lot of people, and if Betty wants that I think we can manage."

I saw Gram look at her daughter in a funny way. "If you'd rather not, Lynn. . . ."

"It's fine, Mother," my mom said, but her heart wasn't in it.

Josh said, "Well, I think a wedding at home is appropriate for an older couple."

Adam smirked. "Well, since Josh approves, I guess everything is all set."

Gram looked across the table at me. "You

haven't said anything, Lizzie. How do you feel about it?"

I wanted to say I thought the whole thing was awful, and I felt Gram had fooled me with all this friend stuff, but I knew if I said anything like that my father would ground me forever. "I guess it's okay," I mumbled.

"Such enthusiasm," my gram said, and I saw the look of concern on her face.

"Okay," Ralph said, rubbing his hands together. "Then, after the ceremony, we could have a small reception at some nice place in town, and invite everyone else we wanted."

I looked at Gram and asked her with a quivering voice, "When is the wedding going to be?"

Gram smiled at Ralph and took his hand. "Well, we thought the beginning of April would be a nice time."

I could hardly believe it! First Gram would get married, and then there would be The Dance. It was *too much* all in one small month.

At that moment the waitress came with our orders, and we went through the whole business of figuring out who got what. My mother crawled under the table to try to get Rose to come out, but she still refused. And Dad barked out, "Lynn, leave her there. Come eat your dinner."

I saw the tears in my mother's eyes when she

lifted her head. I don't know if anyone else did. "She'll starve," Mom sniffed.

"That will be the day," Darcy said. "Josh is right when he calls Rose the Human Garbage Disposal."

"Okay, everyone. Dig in," Dad said, still doing the jovial bit.

I think he was the only one even trying to be happy at the table, except maybe for Ralph.

I guess, Diary, I wasn't what you would call very gracious. I mean, I want Gram to be happy. I really do. But I want to be happy, too. And I don't see how I can if she moves out. Maybe I'm just a very selfish girl. I don't want to be. I want to be a good person. Noble and kind. But it's not easy to do. And I keep thinking, if Gram really, really loved me, would she get married and move away?

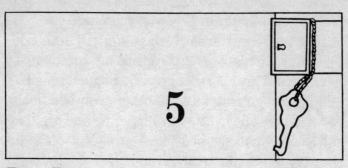

5

Dear **D**iary:

On Saturday night, Ericka and I slept over at Nancy's. I had really been looking forward to it, but it ended up with my feeling that neither of my friends understood me. I can deal with Ericka being a little dense, but Nancy is my best friend, my oldest friend. She should certainly be sympathetic, but she isn't.

I couldn't help talking about Gram's wedding . . . after all, now it's only two months away. "I won't ever get used to the idea of not having Gram around. I really hate Ralph for doing this," I said.

Ericka threw a pillow at me. "It's not just Ralph, you know. Your gram has something to do with this, too. Anyway, I think it's neat. Look, you'll be getting a brand-new grandfather. That sounds like fun to me, so why don't you look at it from that point of view?"

"You just don't understand," I said to Ericka. I turned to Nancy for some comfort.

"I think Ericka is right. All you do is complain.

If I were your gram I'd swat you one."

I turned away from Nancy and got into bed, making sure she was aware that my back was to her. I could hear Ericka opening her sleeping bag and Nancy getting into the other twin bed in the room. Then I heard them whispering and giggling softly for what seemed like hours. Not once did they try to get me to turn around and talk to them. Not once. That's the kind of friends they are.

In the morning I didn't even stay for breakfast, but just biked home. My whole family was in the kitchen eating. "How come you're home so early?" Gram asked.

"I didn't feel like staying. They are nasty, those girls are. Heartless."

"What are they heartless about?" Gram asked.

I was so hurt that I didn't make any effort to watch what I was saying. "Well, they don't un-derstand that it is hard to get used to your . . . your getting married and all. They just don't understand."

Gram stopped eating, and so did Mom. Mom said, "Well, they certainly don't seem very con-siderate. *I* understand."

"I don't," Darcy said.

"Me neither," Adam said.

Then Gram said, as brightly as she could, "How about it if Lizzie and you, Lynn, come and help me pick out a wedding dress on Monday? I think it would be fun."

"I have a meeting of the decorations committee for the dance," I said. It was true, and I hadn't been looking forward to it. But now it seemed like a lifesaver. I didn't want to help Gram look for a wedding dress. It would just hurt too much.

"Well, we can all go together Monday night. A lot of the stores are open."

Mom looked desperate, and I knew she didn't want to go either. "Well, I have to get dinner for everyone and. . . ."

"I'll see to dinner, Lynn," Dad said. "You and Lizzie go with Betty. That sounds great to me."

Then why don't *you* go? I thought. But Dad had that I'll-take-care-of-everything look, and I knew that I was doomed. Mom might get out of this but I wouldn't be able to. And as it turned out, Mom went, too.

I don't know which was worse, the decorations committee meeting or the wedding dress search. The committee met after classes and, of course, Samantha took over. I figured this meeting would take ten minutes. I mean, you talk about balloons and streamers and you go home. Billy Watts, who is the only boy in my class who seems human to me, said, "What do you think, Lizzie?" I was glad that he thought I was knowledgeable about this sort of thing, and so I said with assurance, "No big deal. Balloons and streamers."

Samantha snorted. Really snorted. "*That* is the most immature and unimaginative thing I've ever heard."

I felt my cheeks get red, and I said in a small voice, "What do you have in mind, Samantha?"

"Well, certainly not balloons. After the age of six, they are just stupid. I think we should make some wonderful signs and pictures and maybe have flowers and lights and things like that."

"Wonderful," Candace said.

Candace would have said "wonderful" if Samantha had suggested stringing salamis together. But I have to admit, I wondered why Samantha thought of unusual things and I just thought of balloons. It is obvious why. Samantha is mature and cool and I am a turkey. Will I ever change? Will I ever grow up and be sophisticated?

Billy said, "I don't know. I don't see anything wrong with balloons. Then we can all break them at the end of the dance."

"Brilliant," Samantha said sarcastically. "That would be *great* fun."

Billy just stuck his tongue out at Samantha and walked out of the room. Now why hadn't I at least been able to do that?

"I'll decide what the decorations will be," Samantha said. She took a brush out of her bag and started brushing her long blonde hair, which didn't need brushing at all. She has hair that always looks perfect. "Then I'll give assignments as to what everyone should do to carry out my instructions."

"Who made you queen?" Tanya Malone asked, looking up from the science book she was reading.

I always thought Tanya was nice, but a nerd. But at least she was standing up to Samantha.

"Do *you* have any ideas?" Samantha asked, and Tanya just blushed.

"I don't think I like this committee," Tanya said, and started putting all her books together.

"Well, I'm on *all* the committees," Samantha said, her blue eyes getting very narrow. "Because I'm the only one who really understands about dances."

So that was how *that* went . . . and then there was the shopping expedition with Gram. I think that was worse. We went from store to store, and Gram must have tried on twelve hundred dresses. With each one that she put on, Mom would tilt her head and look at it carefully and then say either, "It isn't the right color," or, "It doesn't hang right," or, "It's too young-looking," or, "It's too old-looking."

Gram looked at me often and asked, "What do you think?"

Most of the time I just said, "I don't know anything about wedding dresses."

Gram was getting impatient. "You don't have to *know* anything. You just have to tell me if it looks good on me or not."

I just shrugged.

Gram looked in the mirror at the dress she had on. She looked beautiful in it . . . she really did. It was a pale blue lacy thing, and it fit her perfectly and made her look tall and thin and lovely. Why couldn't I tell her how pretty she looked? Why couldn't I tell her she was the most beautiful grandmother in the world? But I just couldn't.

Finally Gram turned to the salesperson and said, "I'll take this dress. *I* like it."

So there it was, even more definite. She even had a dress. There were tears in my mother's eyes . . . again. I saw them. Gram saw them. I was as much upset because Mom was upset as I was because Gram was getting married. Mothers aren't supposed to cry because *their* mothers are moving out of the house. Kids do that, not mothers.

When we got home everyone went to their own little piece of space. Gram went up to her apartment. Mom went to her bedroom. And I went into my room. I looked around and remembered when

I had taken Samantha's advice and redecorated my room so that it looked like a 70s disco, and how Gram had helped me put it back to something that looked like *my* room. Now the powder blue walls that Gram and Nancy had helped me paint, which had once comforted me and made me feel safe and secure, just made me want to cry. This was turning out to be the cryingest family! Except, I realized, for Gram. She was strong and determined.

Suddenly I heard loud voices from my mother's room. She and Dad were arguing. "You don't understand," Mom shouted.

"I do," my father yelled back. "I do understand. You're acting like a kid. It's hard enough to accept Lizzie's behavior, much less yours. The only one who is acting her age is Rose. She's a baby, and she's acting like a baby."

He slammed out of their room. I waited a few minutes and then went to the closed door and knocked. "Go away," Mother said, sniffling.

"I want to talk to you," I said, with my mouth pressed against the door.

"Come in," Mom said, blowing her nose. She was sitting on the edge of their bed, looking so sad and forlorn. I went over to her, sat down, and put my arms around her.

"I'm sorry you're so unhappy," I said.

"I'm sorry you are," Mom answered.

"I guess I'm confused," I said. "I mean, I didn't think you'd be so upset. You're a grown-up. It shouldn't be so awful for you to have Gram leave."

Mother sniffled again. "It's just that she's been here so long, and I depend on her for so much, and she's such fun to have around. Your father travels so much and you kids are great, but you're just kids. Gram is someone to talk to."

Then she started crying again, loud, very loud. Baby Rose came into the room, and she joined in the wailing. Darcy came to the door and just yelled, "Shush! The neighbors will think someone died."

Then Gram appeared behind Darcy and looked at us. Rose ran over to her and threw her arms around Gram's legs and hung onto her. "Now you can't go. 'Cause I won't let your legs work."

Gram reached down and gently took Rose's arms from around her legs. Then she walked away. She looked like she felt almost as bad as Mom and I did. I followed her out of the room, but when she heard me behind her she said, "I don't think this is a good time to talk, Lizzie. I just want to be alone."

I couldn't believe it. Gram, who had never not been there for me when I needed her. Ralph sure is changing her!

Oh, by the way, when I saw Nancy in school today she just acted as if nothing had happened

Saturday night. She didn't even apologize or anything . . . and neither did Ericka. But I just figured if they were going to ignore their bad manners, I would be doubly polite and ladylike, and I would ignore their ignoring them . . . if you know what I mean. So we're all talking again. I don't feel exactly great with them, but then I don't feel exactly great any time anymore.

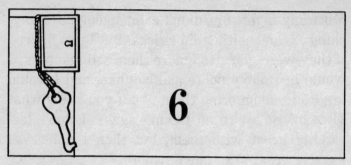

6

Dear **D**iary:

I am dumbstruck, terrified, anxious, and scared. I just realized today that I don't know what kids wear to a dance like the one we're having. I don't *have* anything I want to wear. I don't know who to ask what to wear. *And* I don't know how to dance . . . really. Oh, Nancy and I jump around together sometimes and pretend it's dancing, but I'm not sure it is. And the idea of some boy, even the dumb boys in our class, seeing me hopping around like some kid playing hopscotch is just mortifying.

I have to learn how to dance. And I have to figure out what to wear. Once I would have asked Gram, but I just don't feel that close to her right now. She is so wrapped up in her wedding plans that I don't think she even cares about the rest of us anymore. Except maybe Darcy and Adam, because they're on her side. I thought about talking to Mom, but she's so off in the clouds these days, she wouldn't be much good. And anyway,

Moms don't know much about clothes . . . kids' clothes, that is.

So today I decided to talk to Nancy. After all, what are best friends for? I know she doesn't know *anything* about clothes, but at least I could complain to her. While we were having lunch in the cafeteria, I said with as much confidence as I could gather, "We have to figure out what we are going to wear to the dance, Nancy."

Nancy looked at me as if I had suggested we talk about what we were going to wear at our senior prom. "*I* don't have to figure anything out," Nancy said, shoving a spoonful of orange Jell-O into her mouth. "I'm not going to the dance. Remember?"

I got mad. Real mad. "Nancy Underpeace, *you* are going! If you don't go to the dance, I will *never*, I repeat, *never* go bird-watching with you again. Not as long as I live."

"You hardly ever go with me anyway."

"Well then, I will never *hardly* ever go with you."

And then I began to cry. I know it sounds as if I do nothing but cry, and that isn't so, but lately I sure am doing a lot of it. But to cry in the cafeteria — where anyone could see me, that was gross. Nancy's eyes grew wider and wider as she watched me. She kept patting my arm and wiping my face with her orange-Jell-O-stained napkin.

45

"Don't, Lizzie. Don't! Tell me what's wrong. All I said was — "

I ran outside the cafeteria and found a dark corner to huddle in. Nancy was right on my heels. I just blubbered all over the place. "You say you won't go to the dance. I don't know what to wear. I don't have anyone to ask. I can't dance. And Gram is getting married. My life is a wreck!"

"Okay, okay," Nancy said. "I'll think about the dance. But if I go I'll just stand there. I won't dance, not a step. And you can always ask Samantha what she's going to wear. She used to be your buddy, and you think she's so stylish."

I wiped my face with the back of my hand and snuffled. I tried to smile . . . a little. "Nance, you won't regret it. You'll have a good time. I promise you." I was so glad she was going I could have started dancing right there.

Then I thought about what Nancy had said about asking Samantha what she was wearing to the dance. "I can't ask Samantha. She doesn't even talk to me. I'd really feel like a jerk asking her. But I'll bet she's talking about nothing else. If we just eavesdrop a little, we can get some ideas."

Nancy looked around the cafeteria. "She's sitting over there with Candace. If we sit at the next table we'll be able to hear what they're saying."

I knew Nancy was just trying to distract me,

and that she didn't care a drop about what Samantha and Candace were talking about. And I loved her for doing it. We, as naturally as we could, got our things together and moved to the table next to Samantha. I was right. They were talking about clothes.

"Well," Samantha was saying, "maybe the blue one with a white bottom."

Candace shook her head. "I like the white part, but I think red might look better with it."

Samantha thought for a while and then, brushing that long blonde hair back from her face, said, "Maybe you're right. Or how about khaki and yellow?"

"That's good," Candace answered.

Nancy and I stared at each other. All we were getting was information about colors. But what were the *things* in those colors? What was blue or white or yellow or red? This wasn't helping at all.

Candace stood up. Her dark hair caught the light coming from the fluorescent bulbs, and she really looked great. The fact that she has green eyes doesn't hurt any, either. "Well, I'm going to buy something new. I hate every piece of clothing I own."

"Gre-at idea!" Samantha said. "Let's go shopping Saturday afternoon. I'll pick you up at one, and we'll have lots of time."

They sailed out of the cafeteria without even glancing at Nancy and me. But it was okay, because I had a brilliant idea.

"Nancy, you know what we're going to do?"

"I don't think I want to know."

"We are going to follow them Saturday afternoon. That way we'll see exactly what they buy, and we'll know just what is right to wear."

"No way!" Nancy cried. "*We* are not doing anything. You can if you want, but I am not following those creeps. Never!"

I let my lips tremble a little. A mean, deceitful thing to do, but I wanted Nancy to come with me.

Nancy looked at me and said, "If you cry, Lizzie, I won't talk to you again until we're both thirty-five."

I stopped my trembling and just pouted. "Fine friend you are."

When I got home, the house was silent. My house is never silent. Even when no one is in it, the dog is barking, a radio has been left on, the dishwasher is going, but never silent. I walked into the living room, and Mom was sitting in a chair with Rose in her lap, and they were both sleeping. Gram came into the room and smiled sweetly.

"They look cute, don't they?"

I had to admit they did. "Real cute," I said.

"I'll take Rose up to her room and put her on her bed," Gram said. She leaned over and lifted Rose off of Mom's lap. As she picked her up, Rose opened her eyes, looked at Gram, and started to yell. I mean yell.

"No. You're a bad Gram. I don't want you to pick me up. Lizzie, you do it."

Mom woke up and shook her finger at Rose. "Don't you say that to your gram."

The more she shook her finger, the more Rose yelled. I reached over to her and she threw her arms around me and sobbed, "Nobody loves me anymore. Nobody."

Gram's face was pale. She reached over to pat Rose, but Rose drew back, and Gram left the room. I heard her walking up to her apartment. She didn't even come down to dinner. And Diary, that was the quietest, saddest dinner we have almost ever had.

When we had finished eating, Gram came down and pulled a chair over to the table. "I have just been talking to Ralph. I have decided that getting married is not such a good idea after all. So I've told him that the wedding is off."

I guess I really am a terrible person, but I have to admit I felt this flash of happiness go through me at Gram's words. She wasn't going to leave after all. We would all be together, just like always.

"Betty," Dad said, "you can't do that. You and Ralph love each other."

Gram just sighed wearily. "I can't upset this family any more. Lizzie and Lynn go around crying all the time. And Rose won't even let me touch her. My own little grandchild and she won't let me near her. I just can't cause this kind of unhappiness to my family."

Everyone was silent. I knew I should say, "Marry him, Gram. It's okay." But I couldn't, and I didn't. Rose slipped off her chair and went over to Gram and crawled up into her lap. "You mean you'll be staying right here?"

Gram hugged Rose. "Right here."

Everyone was quiet except Dad, who kept saying, "Betty, this isn't right. You can't give up your life for us."

"That's not what I'm doing, Bob. I'm just giving up Ralph."

Darcy grew wide-eyed. "You mean you won't even see him anymore?"

"I don't think so, Darcy," Gram said.

Mom got up and went over to Gram. She put her arms around her and whispered, "I don't know what to say. I can't deny I'm glad you're not leaving us, but . . ."

"There's nothing to say, Lynn, dear," Gram said. "And you, Lizzie, what do you have to say?"

I couldn't stop myself, I was glad, relieved. I

50

felt safe again. "Everything will be fun again, Gram. We'll have good times together and laugh and everything. You'll see."

Gram kissed my cheek. "I'm tired. I'll just run along to bed."

I listened to her going up the stairs. Her step was heavy, not like Gram's at all. But I know things will be fine. We'll go to the mall and go to the movies. We'll have our talks together. I'll ask her what to wear to the dance, and maybe she'll even come with Nancy and me on Saturday. We were so happy together before Ralph. After all, she's known us much longer than she's known him.

I hope being glad Gram isn't going to marry Ralph doesn't make me a bad person. It isn't as if I want her to be unhappy. I just want her happy the way we used to be.

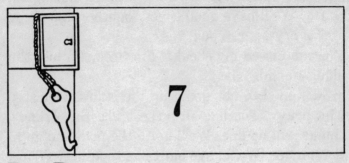

7

Dear **D**iary:

I couldn't wait to tell Nancy about Gram the next day. As soon as I saw her waiting on the corner for me (we always go to school together) I raced over to her. "Gram isn't marrying Ralph after all."

Nancy was startled. "He ditched her?"

I was really mad. "Of course *he* didn't ditch *her*. *She* ditched *him*." Nancy could be so stupid sometimes. As if any man in his right mind would ditch my gram.

"Why?" Nancy asked. "I thought she loved him."

"I guess she loves us more," I said, feeling very smug.

Nancy just looked thoughtful. "Was it some kind of contest?"

We'd been walking slowly, but I just stopped. "What do you mean by that?"

Nancy stopped walking, too. "Well, you sound

like she couldn't love all of you and still be married to Ralph."

"I don't think I want to walk with you, Nancy. You don't seem to understand anything."

Nancy just shrugged. "Maybe this is all too grown-up for me. All this getting married stuff. I just don't see why your gram can't marry Ralph and still be your gram."

We kept on walking, but I stayed a good few feet away from Nancy. "Of course she'd be my gram. I didn't say she wouldn't be, but she would be a different kind of gram. Anyway, obviously she wants to stay with us, and that's what she's going to do."

I know I sounded really snippy, but I was just tired of Nancy, my best friend, not getting what I was talking about half the time.

"You sure are sensitive these days," Nancy said. "If you go back to being the old Lizzie, I don't care what your gram does."

I moved closer to Nancy and grabbed her arm. "I'm going to ask Gram if she wants to go to the mall with us Saturday and see what Samantha buys."

Nancy buttoned the blazer she was wearing over a gray sweatshirt. "Lizzie, I think you've gone bananas. Why would your gram want to go to the mall to follow Samantha around? *I* don't even want to."

I looked at Nancy and narrowed my eyes, very deliberately. "She *loves* to go to the mall. You know that. She loves being with you and me. And you have on the weirdest outfit I have ever seen. Who wears a blazer over a sweatshirt?"

"I do," Nancy said. She looked a little hurt, and I began to feel guilty. "And it's one thing," Nancy went on, "to go to the mall with you and me, and another to follow Samantha and Candace around. *That* is a very immature thing to do."

"If you are saying I am immature, you have another say coming. You're the immature one. You don't even want to go to the dance. You don't even want to buy anything to wear. You don't even want to learn how to dance." I ran away, leaving Nancy staring after me. I could just feel her eyes on my back.

Well, Nancy was right about one thing. Gram didn't want to go to the mall with us. I went up to her apartment to ask her. She looked a little pale, and she had rings under her eyes, neither of which is like Gram at all. I was sure she'd be cheered up by my suggestion.

"I don't think so, Lizzie," was what she said. "And I think there might be a better way to figure out what to wear than following Samantha around."

I was disappointed that Gram wasn't coming with us, but I didn't say anything about it. I did ask, "What's wrong with following Samantha?"

"Well, first of all you are different types. What looks good on Samantha might not look good on you. And secondly, if she sees you following her she's going to be very nasty about it."

Then she just looked away from me and said, "But you do what you want, Lizzie." Then she picked up a magazine and started to read.

She never did anything like that when I was with her, just turn away from me and read. I felt tears gathering in my eyes, and I didn't want her to see it so I started for the door. I knew she'd call me back . . . but she didn't. At the door I turned to look at her, and she wasn't reading anymore. She was just staring out the window.

On Friday I worked out the plan for Saturday's trip to the mall with Nancy. Or rather, Nancy listened while I planned.

"First we'll hang around the bus stop near Candace's house, so we can ride to the mall with them and make sure we know where they go."

Nancy said with great disinterest, "How do you know they won't bike to the mall?"

"I know. They aren't going to ride their bikes when they may end up with a lot of packages. So just meet me at the bus stop a little before one. Remember, Samantha said she'd pick Candace up at one?"

"This is going to be a disaster. I know it," Nancy said.

Well, Diary, it was not one of my better ideas. I have to admit that. It started out all right, except that Nancy was grumbling right from the start — and when Nancy grumbles, she really grumbles. She's not one of those one-little-grumble-and-then-cheers-up girls. She just keeps at it. We met at the bus stop near Candace's house, and we just sort of hovered around, trying to look as if we weren't waiting for anything besides the bus, until Samantha and Candace appeared.

Samantha is no dummy, and I think she knew something was up. She looked at me with that haughty look of hers and asked, "What are *you* doing here?"

"We're waiting for the bus. It *is* a bus stop," I answered, trying to sound just as haughty. But actually, haughty isn't my thing. I think I have to put that on my list of things to learn.

"How come you're not waiting at *your* bus stop?" Candace asked. Now, Candace *is* the dummy type, and I wished she hadn't picked that moment to smarten up. But we were saved by the bell, or rather the bus, because it came along at that second.

We all piled on and Nancy pulled me to the back, away from Samantha and Candace. I would have sat right near them and tried to listen to whatever they were talking about, but I guess Nancy has more integrity than I do. She finds it hard to be dishonest, and I guess I don't . . . at least sometimes. When we got to the mall we all got out, and I started trailing after Samantha. She turned around, glared at me, and said, still haughty, "Are you following us?"

Believe it or not, Nancy saved me. Nancy is really a good friend, even when she doesn't want to be. *"This,"* she said, "is a mall. Open to everyone. It's a free country, and we have as much right to be here as you do."

Nancy has never said one word to Samantha before, and Samantha was so startled, she just took Candace's hand and pulled her along.

Nancy shook her head at me with disgust. "If we are going to follow those two, at least we have to do it carefully. *You* are as obvious as a red flag. Honestly, Lizzie, try to remember your private eye movies on TV."

I had to agree I wasn't very good at this. But we just stayed yards and yards behind Samantha and watched what they were doing. They looked in every store window along the way, even the sporting goods store, and those two girls aren't into sports. I finally figured out they were looking in to see if any boys they knew were there. Samantha was especially interested in trying to find Kevin Eckert, the cutest boy in the sixth grade. Or at least most girls think Kevin is. I personally don't think he's half as cute as Billy Watts.

Finally they went into Milliken's, which is this great, really cool store for teenage types. I go in there a lot, but I never know what to buy. I get so confused by all the stuff. Samantha and Candace didn't seem confused at all. With great determination, as if they were about to climb Mt. Everest or something equally important, they marched to the rear of the store. Nancy and I walked after them, stopping at different counters along the way, so that we seemed to be shopping, too. I was terrified that Samantha would turn around and see us, but she was too busy. She pushed clothes around on the racks; took some things out and held them up against her; shook her head and put them back. I thought everything would look wonderful on her, but she obviously thought differently. Sometimes she would pull a skirt out, and Candace would shake her head vigorously, No. How did they know so much? How could they be so sure that one thing was right and another wrong? It all looked great to me.

I found a rack of blouses nearby, and I started doing what Samantha had done. I pulled out one after another and held them up against me. I then looked at Nancy for an answer. But Nancy just shrugged at all of them. "I don't know," she said. "Why ask me? You know I don't know."

Nancy can be such a pain sometimes. I was really angry at her. And yet, why should I expect her to be a fashion expert when I certainly am not, and Nancy is less interested in clothes than I am? Less interested is a dumb thing to write. Nancy isn't interested at all. Like, at that moment, she was wearing jeans with holes in both knees and a down jacket that had a paint streak across the front. I couldn't even think about where she had been that was being painted. But Nancy can get messy if she is within ten blocks of dirt.

I looked over at Samantha and saw that she and Candace were going to the the dressing room with a pile of clothes over their arms. I grabbed things off the racks without even looking, whispered at Nancy to come on, and ran after Samantha. Milliken's is one of those stores that has a huge try-on room that everyone goes into. It's kind of fun watching what everyone else is putting on. But today all I cared about was Samantha.

She immediately took off her jeans and sweater, and she had on the most *wonderful* underwear. Even Nancy stared. Who else would have on a bra and panties that had teddy bears printed on them? And teddy bears in all different colors. If I had underwear like that I would hardly care what went over it. I was really embarrassed to have to take off my clothes and let the world see white cotton pants, not even the bikini type, but just plain old underpants, and a camisole. I don't even wear a bra yet. But if I wanted to seem to be trying on clothes I had to take mine off. I thought about just putting new things over what I was wearing, but I knew that was ridiculous.

I was really in trouble, because I hadn't even bothered to look at sizes or colors or anything when I had grabbed the clothes off the racks. So there I was in a blouse that was two sizes too big and pants that were so small I couldn't zip them up. Nancy put her hand over her mouth so she wouldn't laugh, and I gave her one of those one-word-out-of you looks.

Samantha looked at me and smiled a mean smile. "Very chic, Lizzie. It's you . . . really you."

She had on a pink wool skirt and a white sweater that had little roses on it. She looked gorgeous with her blonde hair reaching her shoulders. That's it, I thought, pink and white. And little flowers. But then she pulled the things off and said to Candace, "It's just a little tacky." It didn't seem tacky to me at all. It seemed great. I kept staring as she put on tight yellow pants and a pale blue blouse. That looked even better. I couldn't take my eyes off her.

"Chill it," Nancy said. "You look so obvious. Try something else on."

I pulled off the shirt and pants and put on a khaki skirt that reached the floor and a sweatshirt that reached my knees. Now you know I'm short . . . so I guess I don't have to say anything more. Nancy just burst out laughing. "You look like a little kid trying on her mother's clothes."

How could I hate Nancy at that moment? Looking in the mirror made me laugh, too.

Then Samantha was gone again. I was about to follow her outside, when Nancy pointed out that she had left Candace to guard her clothes, so Samantha was going to return. Which she did. This time she tried on an outfit that I would have died to be able to wear, but never could. She slipped into tight black pants with stirrups that went under her feet. She couldn't have put a feather under those pants without it showing. Over the pants she wore a loose black cotton sweater. She brushed her blonde hair until it gleamed more than usual and examined herself in the mirror. Everyone in that try-on room was looking at Samantha . . . and she knew it. She turned and twisted and looked at herself from every angle in the mirror.

"You look good, kid," a woman who was trying on clothes a few feet away said.

Even Candace was gazing at Samantha with envy, and Candace doesn't have anything to feel self-conscious about in the looks department. "I think I'll get the same thing in a different color," she said.

"You do," Samantha said meanly, "and I'll never speak to you again. Never."

Candace didn't.

Nancy and I left the mall. I didn't buy anything because I felt nothing would look good on me after seeing Samantha in her black outfit. I could hardly speak all the way home, I felt so jealous.

I guess Gram is right, Samantha and I are different types. I just wish I knew what type I was.

8

Dear Diary:

Something has happened in our house. I'm not even sure what it is, but things are different. I thought we'd all be so happy. Gram isn't getting married. We're all going to stay together, but I don't feel we're very together right now. Gram stays in her room a lot when she's home. Often she doesn't even come down and have dinner with us. She just fixes something in her own apartment . . . and I don't think she fixes much. I see half-eaten TV dinners in her garbage. Now please don't think I'm the kind of creep who goes through other people's garbage. But once in a while, when I'm putting ours in the cans in the garage, I can't help seeing what's there already. That's when I see Gram's TV dinners.

Dad looks at Mom and me as if we have committed some crime, and he sighs a lot. Darcy and Adam talk about reading articles in magazines about selfishness and lack of consideration, and what awful traits they are. I know they are talking about me . . . and Mom, too. Josh is so involved with his girlfriend, Jennifer, he doesn't even know we're alive. And Rose keeps waiting for Gram to come down and play with her. We sure are a cheery lot.

Last night the lady who owns the real estate agency where Gram works came over to go over some business with Gram. When she came downstairs, she came into the living room, where most of us were watching TV. Ms. Markowitz, the lady, got right to the point. "Betty sure isn't her old self anymore."

Mom cleared her throat nervously. "What do you mean?"

Ms. Markowitz looked Mom right in the eyes. "Well, since Betty stopped seeing Ralph she is quiet, distracted, pale, and doesn't even eat much. That's what I mean."

"It was her decision," Mom said.

"Was it?" Ms. Markowitz asked. "Sometimes people make decisions because they are very kind-hearted and don't want to hurt the people they love, who are acting like children." With that she just walked out the door.

"That was a very rude thing to say," Mom said.

"I agree," I replied.

"Sometimes the truth hurts," Dad answered, and he walked out, too.

I thought about what Ms. Markowitz had said

as I lay in bed. And then I realized that I had just not been trying hard enough to amuse Gram. After all, she had been seeing Ralph so much, and now she had free time. I would just have to make sure she was busy every minute. I got out of bed and ran up the stairs to Gram's place. I knocked on her door and then went in. She was brushing her hair, and I said, "How about going to the movies Friday night? Maybe we could even have a hamburger somewhere first, and then we could go for ice cream afterwards. And Saturday afternoon we could go bird-watching with Nancy, and Saturday night we could. . . ."

Gram smiled . . . a little. "Hold it, Lizzie! Let's just see how I feel when the weekend comes. I've been tired lately, and your schedule seems too much for me."

I wanted to say something else, but I didn't know what to say. Then I remembered Samantha. "You were right, Gram. Samantha's style is different than mine. Only, I don't know what mine is. What do you think? What type do you think I am?"

Gram looked at me carefully, almost as if I were a stranger. "I'm not sure, Lizzie, who you are. I guess you'll have to find out as you go along."

I was so hurt that I just left the room. How could she say that? She didn't know what type I was? Something inside me made me think Gram wasn't talking about my clothes type, that she meant much more. I felt cold as I went to my room. And scared, too. I got into bed and just lay there, worrying. What did Gram mean? I needed her so badly at that minute, needed just to have her put her arms around me and tell me she loved me, that I ran back upstairs.

When I got to her door, I heard her . . . crying. My gram was crying. I had never, never seen her cry . . . or even heard her cry. I couldn't believe it! But I had to because I was hearing her with my very own ears, which I had washed that morning. I ran down to the kitchen, where Mom and Dad were having tea.

"Gram is crying. I was outside her door, and I heard her."

Mom frowned. "Are you sure, Lizzie?"

"I'm positive."

Dad turned to Mom. "Are you surprised, Lynn?"

I sat down at the table and put my head down on my arms. "She's not the same at all. It's like my gram is gone. She's here but she isn't my gram."

Mom patted my head. "I know. She isn't the same, is she?"

"What are we going to do?" I lifted my head and looked at Dad.

Dad sighed, for a change. "I think you and your

mother had better think this over tonight. Maybe by morning you'll know what you have to do."

But Diary, I knew. I really knew right then what I was going to have to do.

This morning when I woke up I had this awful, heavy feeling. Dad had left for work, but I could hear Mom moving around in their bedroom. I went in and sat down on the bed.

Mom came over and sat next to me and took my hand. "I guess we've both been very selfish. I should have acted like a grown-up. You should have acted like a semi grown-up. The only one who had a right to act like a baby was Rose. Because she is a baby. Your father was right. If we want the mother and the grandmother we both loved, we have to let her go, Lizzie. It's as simple as that."

"I know," I said in a whisper. "I knew that last night. You go up and tell Gram that we want her to marry Ralph."

Mom got up and began to comb her hair. "I don't think so, Lizzie. I think you have to go up and tell her that. If I tell her that it's what we both want she won't believe me. She'll accept my feelings, but she'll worry about yours."

I could hardly stand the thought of having to talk to Gram . . . after I'd been so awful. She was sure to hate me. I didn't want to face that. "I can't, Mom. I just can't."

"You didn't find it impossible to let her know you *didn't* want her to get married. So I guess you can find a way to tell her you *do*."

I walked up the stairs right then and there, before I lost the little nerve I had. I knocked on Gram's door and when she said, "Come in," I did.

She was putting polish on her nails. I remembered how, when I was a real little kid, she would polish my nails and then put a spot on the tip of my nose. I went over to her and sat down on the floor next to her feet.

"Gram . . . I've been thinking . . . about Ralph, that is. . . ."

Gram stopped the polishing. "I think everything has been said about Ralph that needs to be said."

"No. That's not true. I've been awful, a brat, a thoughtless, selfish brat."

Gram looked at me, waiting for me to go on.

I looked right into her eyes. "I'm sorry. I want you to marry Ralph. So does Mom. We want you to be happy, and we want you to forgive us, but mostly we want you to be happy."

There were tears in Gram's eyes. "And what about your happiness? I'll move out of this house. Just a few miles away, but still out of this house."

"I'll be happy Gram, if you go back to being the way you were. Laughing and joking and going to the mall with me. Can we still go to the mall together?" I was suddenly worried.

Gram laughed, loud and hard. Her old laugh. "We can go to the mall and the movies. You can sleep over at my house, and we can talk half the night, if you want. Things will be different, Lizzie, but better. And . . . if you want one . . . you'll have a grandfather, too."

I put my head on Gram's knee. "Ralph must hate me. He must hate Mom and Rose and me."

Gram stroked my head. "No. He doesn't at all. He understood. He wasn't happy, and he didn't agree with my decision, but he understood. Ralph is like that. You'll see."

"I hope so, Gram. I never hated Ralph, just the idea of your leaving."

Gram stood up and pushed me to the door. "Now you just let me have me a little privacy, and I'll give Ralph a call. I'll be down in a little while."

I went to the kitchen, where Mom was fixing breakfast, and we sat together and waited. It seemed like ages before Gram came down . . . smiling.

"Well, I think I'll make a pretty nice April bride, don't you? And you, Lizzie, will make a beautiful bridesmaid. That is, if you would honor me by being my attendant."

Then we were all hugging each other and kissing and laughing and crying. The rest of the kids came down, and we had to explain everything to them. Rose was about to protest when Mom just looked at her and said, "Behave!"

And she did.

Can you imagine, Diary, I am going to be Gram's bridesmaid. I am so excited I can hardly sit still. At first I thought Mom might be hurt . . . you know, that Gram didn't pick her. But she wasn't at all. She just immediately started talking about what I was going to wear. Now I have *another* outfit to worry about. It's all too much.

Tonight I went into Darcy's room and stood over her desk, where she was doing her homework. "Darc, is it okay with you? I mean, about me being the bridesmaid. I mean, are you hurt or insulted or anything?"

Darcy looked up and said, "No. I'm not. After all, you are the oldest granddaughter. And . . . I've always known Gram liked you the best. I mean, I know she loves me, too. And she loves me enough, too, but you're her favorite girl in the family. It's okay. I'm Mom's favorite."

I was stunned. "You *are*?"

Darcy looked very casual and very calm. "Sure. Haven't you noticed?"

I went back to my room and thought about that. She was right. I had noticed, but just never really let myself put it into words. I guess it all equals out in the end. I know Mom loves me, and I don't know what there is about Darcy that does make her Mom's favorite girl. Maybe because she's so logical, like Mom. But then I don't know what makes me Gram's favorite. And I guess the reasons don't really matter. Except why is it that people have favorites in the first place? Is it like some kind of law of nature or something? I'll have to talk to Adam about that. He's my favorite.

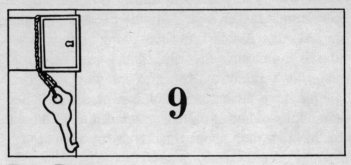

9

Dear Diary:

I'm a wreck, an absolute wreck. No eleven-year-old should have to deal with two such tremendous firsts coming one right after the other. It will be the first time I have ever been a bridesmaid, and the first dance I will ever have gone to. I need a dress for the wedding, something for the dance, and also I have to learn how to dance so that if I make a fool of myself with what I wear, at least I won't make a fool of myself by the way I dance.

I finally decided to ask Adam to show me how to dance. Like I said, or maybe I didn't — that's the thing about keeping a diary, I'm never sure what I've told you and what I haven't, and I just don't have the time to keep rereading what I've already written. So if I repeat myself, please understand.

Anyway, I'm not afraid of the fast dances. I can jump around okay for those. But what if they play some slow dances? I mean, there I am really scared! Do I put my cheek against the boy's cheek? Do I put my arm around his neck? Do I want to do a slow dance with any boy? Well, maybe Billy. Just maybe, Diary.

Well, at first Adam kicked and screamed and said he wasn't dancing with any sister. Did I ever say he was my favorite? I must have been out of my mind. Well, Mom heard him yelling at me and came in and insisted he teach me. You can imagine how great that made our first lesson. Adam was mad. He grabbed me as if he were going to strangle me instead of dance with me. He put his arm around my waist, but loosely, as if I were contaminated in some way. It didn't make me feel exactly confident.

Nancy came in at that moment and sat down to watch us. That made me feel even worse. She didn't say a word . . . just watched. Like we were some kind of science experiment.

"Lizzie!" Adam shouted. "Take your arm from around my neck! You're choking me! Put your hand on my shoulder! Now just follow me. Whatever the boy does, you just do, too. And try to be, well, graceful I guess."

Nancy snickered, and I turned and glared at her. Graceful, I thought. If I knew I could be graceful I wouldn't be panicked. I shuffled around with Adam and tried not to lean on him too hard when I stumbled, which was every few steps.

He dropped his arm from around my waist and said, "You're terrible, Lizzie. You're not following." He looked at Nancy. "Come on. Maybe if she watches us she'll loosen up."

Nancy bolted from her chair and practically cowered in a corner of the den, where we were practicing. "Not me!" Nancy said.

"Come on, Nance. Don't be a jerk. I need to watch you," I said. "I'll go bird-watching with you if you dance with Adam."

"Promise?" Nancy asked.

"Promise," I answered.

She got up and went over to Adam. They were exactly the same height and looked kind of nice together. Adam put his arm around her waist and said what he'd said to me: "Follow me." The amazing thing was that Nancy did. She could follow. I was mad. "You've been practicing somewhere without me," I said accusingly.

Nancy looked over her shoulder and said, "Never!"

"So how come you can dance?" I asked.

Nancy shrugged. Her face was flushed but she looked like she was almost enjoying herself, though I knew she would never admit it. "I don't know," she said. "I must be a natural talent."

Adam dropped his arm and said to me, "Okay.

That's how you should do it. Good luck." Then he left the room.

I went over to Nancy and said, "Can you lead, too? With all that 'natural talent,' you probably can. Try, and I'll try to follow you."

"This isn't a good idea," Nancy said. "I know we are going to fight. I just know it."

And she was right. She couldn't lead and I still couldn't follow. And all we did was accuse each other of being clumsy, klutzy, and uncooperative. Finally Nancy said, "I'm going home. Who needs this? I may not even go to the dance."

I went up to my room and threw myself on the bed. I was hopeless. If they do play slow dances, and any boy happens to ask me to dance, I will cripple him. No doubt. I was feeling cold, so I went over to my closet and opened the door to get out a sweater. I stepped back as I pulled the door open. That gave me the idea. Who needed Adam or Nancy? I put on my radio and flipped the dial until I found a dreamy slow tune. Then I grabbed hold of the closet doorknob and danced back and forth. As I pulled the door open, I danced backwards. As I shut the door, I danced forward. It all worked wonderfully. I felt like I could even dance with Patrick Swayze. If I could just take the door to the dance with me, I'd be fine.

Suddenly I knew someone was watching me.

Gram was standing in my room, and she had a hand covering her mouth, but her eyes told me she was laughing. "Don't laugh," I warned her.

"Who's laughing?" she asked. "You and the door make a gorgeous couple."

"Very funny," I muttered.

Gram held her arms out to me. "Slow dances I can do. Come on. I'll dance with you. I'm certainly as good as a closet door."

Reluctantly I walked into her arms. I mean, she's a grandmother, what could she know about dancing? But she did. Her hand was firm on my back, and she carefully led me where she wanted to go. And I could follow her, too. I suddenly knew something very important. For a girl to dance well with a boy, the boy had to know how to dance, too. He had to be able to lead, or no girl could follow. I felt like running downstairs, finding Adam, and yelling "Learn how to lead."

So, Diary, if I'm lucky enough to dance with a boy who can let me know the direction he intends to go in, I'll be all right. If I get an Adam, I'm in trouble. But what I want to know is this — how come Nancy could follow him?

On top of everything else, Samantha is being her usual awful self. In the cafeteria today, she came over to the table where Nancy and Ericka and I were eating. "So, have you decided what you are going to wear to the dance? Or are you just going to buy what you saw me buying? I know you were spying on me."

It's hard to be indignant when someone is telling the truth, but Nancy looked at Samantha and said, "Elizabeth has more important things to buy than something for a stupid sixth-grade dance. *She* is going to be the bridesmaid at her grandmother's wedding and is going to wear a most beautiful dress. Better than anything you have ever owned."

I could see that Samantha was silenced for a minute. *She* had never been a bridesmaid, that was obvious. I smiled gratefully at Nancy. What a friend!

And I did get the most beautiful dress for the wedding. Mom met me after school today, and we went shopping. I tried on one dress after another and felt like an overdressed flower garden in every one of them. "Maybe I'm not the bridesmaid type," I said.

"There is no bridesmaid type," Mom answered. "Anyone can be a bridesmaid, even you."

She looked at the pink taffeta dress I had on and shook her head wearily. Then she glanced at my feet. "You know, Lizzie, it doesn't help any that you have on filthy sneakers, one with a hole in the toe. You could have worn appropriate shoes."

"I don't *have* appropriate shoes," I answered, just as wearily as she.

"True," she replied. "We have to dress you from your underwear out."

"Right," I agreed eagerly. "Teddy bear underwear is what I want. Teddy bears."

"What's with this teddy bear business?" Mom asked. "I know just what we are going to get, if we ever find a dress for you."

But we did find a dress. It is pale, pale yellow. It's simple and made out of a nice silky material. It has a little Peter Pan collar, and long sleeves, and it falls in these really soft folds to below my knees. I love it. And I love my underwear, too. It has roses on it, but you know, roses are better for a wedding than teddy bears. Not, Diary, that I think anyone is going to see my underwear, but you know what I mean. And Mom bought me pumps with a real little heel, too. I can't believe how I look.

Anyway, Diary, as you can imagine, no one is talking about anything but the wedding. Gram wanted the ceremony here, in our house, but that turned out to be impossible. Between the children and the animals and the piles of laundry always waiting to be carried upstairs, you couldn't possibly have a wedding here. So we are going to have the ceremony at Ralph's house. His daughter

Josie, who lives nearby, is going to take care of all the arrangements. Josie is nice enough. She has a five-year-old little boy, and a baby.

Ralph's house is perfect for a wedding. It's neat and decorated, if you know what I mean. You can tell only one person has been living in all that space. And a person without animals, too. Chairs are going to be set up in his living room, and I'll even have a little aisle to walk down. I'm sure I'm going to trip or faint or sneeze or something. Gram and I practiced the other night at Ralph's. Gram went upstairs to put on her high heels so she'd know exactly how she'd feel on the big day, and Ralph and I were alone. I felt really uptight. I mean, what do you say to a step-grandfather-to-be? But you know what? He came over to me and said, "Thank you, Lizzie."

"For what?" I asked.

"For telling your gram to marry me. For making her know you'd like it to happen. It was a very mature, unselfish thing to do."

I was so flabbergasted. Ralph was talking to me just like I was a grown-up. But I had to be honest with him. "It wasn't exactly unselfish. I mean, I was miserable because Gram was miserable. I wanted to feel good, too."

"Well," Ralph said, "we often do things that make other people happy that happen to make us happy, too. There's nothing wrong with that."

"I guess not," I said. It was then that I noticed that Ralph has the warmest, bluest, nicest eyes. He really is a good person.

"Lizzie, I hope someday you'll be able to think of me as your grandfather, not just the man who married your gram."

I smiled and felt melty inside. "You know, Ralph, I think that is very possible."

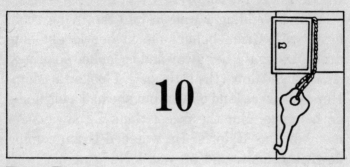

10

Dear **D**iary:

Well, Gram got married today. I can't believe that she's gone, but she is.

This morning when I woke up, I had such an empty feeling in my stomach, because I knew this was the last morning I'd wake up with her in the house. Oh, I know, she said I could sleep over at her house sometimes. But that will be different. I almost didn't want to get out of bed and have the day start. I wanted to just lie there and pretend it was a day just like any other one. But I heard all the noise in the house, and Gram laughing, and people running up and down the stairs, so I had to get up.

I have to admit, Diary, when I got all dressed for the wedding, I really looked pretty. The dress was just right, and I carried a little bouquet of yellow and white flowers, and had a matching circlet to wear in my hair. I had practiced walking around in my heels enough so that I wasn't too worried that I'd fall over.

At the wedding I walked into the living room first, with Gram behind me in her lovely blue dress. Dad gave her away and he looked so proud. As I walked down the little aisle, I looked at Mom. Her eyes were kind of wet, but she had a big smile on her face. But the face I think I'll always remember was Ralph's. He watched Gram coming down the aisle, and he was looking at her with such love and such admiration that it almost took my breath away. I wonder if, someday, some man will ever look at me like that. I hope so, and I would like to look at him the way Gram looked at Ralph when she reached his side. She was smiling and gazing deep into his eyes. It was the most romantic moment I have ever seen. Who says that older people can't be just as romantic as young ones?

The ceremony was the usual, lovely one. At least, Mom said it was the usual one. I've never been to a wedding before. After it was over, there was much hugging and kissing, and then we all went to the best hotel in town, where there was a big reception, and all the people who hadn't been able to fit into Ralph's house were there, too. I think I forgot to mention that Gram invited Nancy to the whole thing, ceremony and reception. That is so Gram. First of all, to want Nancy there. And second of all, to know I would feel happy to have her there.

Anyway, the party was wonderful, with delicious food and a little band that played, and lots more hugging and kissing. Gram danced the first dance with Ralph, and how they glided around the room! You know, Ralph is graceful. Then she danced with Dad, and then with Josh, and then Adam. It was so sweet. Then Ralph asked me to dance. Like Gram, he's a good dancer, and I could even follow him. Maybe that says something about how I'll do at the school dance. But then those boys probably aren't as good as Ralph.

After a couple of hours, Gram and Ralph got ready to go on their honeymoon. They're going to California. So far away. Gram threw her bouquet, and a lady in the real estate agency caught it and there was a lot of laughing and joking. So now Gram's really gone.

The house felt so empty when I went to bed. When I thought of her apartment upstairs without her in it, I wanted to cry. But when I thought of how happy she looked, I wanted to smile. Mom came in and sat on the edge of my bed for a while and held my hand.

"Are you okay?" she asked.

"I miss her already," I answered.

She nodded. "I know. Me, too, but she'll be back

from her honeymoon in two weeks, and then she'll be just a few miles away from us. It will be different, but she'll always be your gram."

Then she kissed me and went out of the room. I noticed that she left my bed lamp on, as if she knew I wouldn't want to be in the dark.

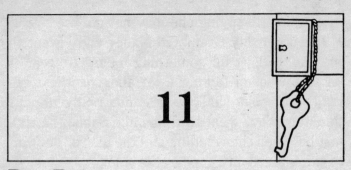

11

Dear **D**iary:

I know it's been a long time since I wrote last
. . . almost three weeks. But I guess I was trying
to adjust to Gram's being gone, and I felt too bad
to write. I missed her soooo much. A couple of
times I just went up to her apartment and sat in
her chair. The rooms still smelled of her perfume,
and all her favorite books and records were there.
I just sat in the quiet and tried to pretend she
would be walking in any second. But you know,
I couldn't believe it at all. I knew she was gone.

Now that she is back from her trip, she is going
to move all her things to her new home. I don't
know what we'll do with the apartment. I have
this fantasy that Mom will let me move up there,
but can you imagine how all the other kids would
react to that? Especially since they are still shar-
ing rooms and I have one of my own.

Anyway, now that Gram is back, I think I'll get
used to her being married. The next thing on my
agenda is to get ready for the dance. Nancy, of

course, is still saying she may not go.

The other day Gram and Nancy and I went to the mall to look for something for me to wear. I know I've been talking a lot about clothes. I'm really not that shallow. I'm not really *always* thinking about what to wear, like Samantha. It's just between the wedding and the dance, I've *had* to think about my appearance a lot.

Nancy came with us just to watch, she said. I don't think she would have come at all, but Gram talked her into it. So off we went. As Gram was driving us to the mall, I said, "Samantha is wearing these great black pants. I'd like something like that."

Gram didn't take her eyes off the road. "Well, Lizzie, let's see. Black pants may look fine on Samantha, but I'm not sure they're right for you."

"I don't think they're right for her at all," Nancy shot back.

"Nancy, I didn't ask for your opinion," I said.

"You're too short for those black pants," Nancy went right on.

"In other words, Samantha looks great in them, but I'd look awful."

"Sort of like that," Nancy answered, not even realizing she was being insulting.

"You know," I said, "you are the most outspoken person I know. And sometimes a person shouldn't be."

Nancy was about to answer me back when Gram said, "Okay, the both of you, just stop. This is supposed to be an afternoon we are going to enjoy. Don't fight."

I stuck my tongue out at Nancy, and she stuck hers back out at me. I knew we were acting like three-year-olds, but I didn't care.

We parked the car and walked to Milliken's, and as soon as we got into the store I felt confused. There was just so much, and I still had no idea of what kind of image I wanted. That's what I've been thinking about lately, creating a new image, just like they do in all the magazines. But it's hard to do when I'm not sure what image I have now. Anyway, we just roamed up and down the aisles until we came to this rack of skirts. Gram stopped and picked one out. It was a blue cotton skirt with white polka dots on it. I couldn't believe that she thought it would look good on me. But she put it over her arm and then found a white blouse with puffed sleeves and took that, too. We all trooped into the try-on room, and I put on the skirt and blouse. It didn't look anything like black pants, and I was about to take it off, when Gram grabbed hold of my arm. "Look in the mirror again, Lizzie. Look at Lizzie, not Samantha."

I did. And I had to admit I looked good. Not at all like Samantha, and not much like the Lizzie I knew, but I liked the girl staring back at me.

Nancy nodded her head, "You look good, Lizzie. Buy the stuff and let's go."

As we walked to the cashier's line, Gram stopped and said very casually. "Look at those jeans, Nancy. Aren't they attractive?"

They were a kind of gray denim with really slim legs. Nancy looked, too. "They're nice, I guess."

"Why don't you try them on, Nancy?" Gram said.

"I don't have any money with me, and I don't need the jeans," Nancy said, and she started to walk away.

Gram took Nancy's arm. "I'd like to buy them for you. As a pre-birthday present. And I'm sure you could use another pair of jeans."

As she was talking she was also picking a red shirt off a rack. Again, we all trooped into the dressing room, and this time Nancy put on the clothes Gram had picked out. The jeans fit her perfectly. I think they were the first jeans I'd ever seen on Nancy that didn't look too big. And the red shirt was terrific with her blonde hair.

"Okay," Gram said, "I'm going to buy them both. I'm sure you'll find some place to wear them."

Since Nancy's birthday wasn't for another three months, I knew what Gram was doing, and I hoped it worked. Maybe if Nancy had the great clothes, which looked so good on her, she might get a little more confidence and go to the dance. I don't think Gram can work miracles, but who knows?

After we shopped we had a soda, and then I went home with Gram . . . to her home, I mean. It seems so funny that her home isn't my home. But I was going to have dinner with her and Ralph, and sleep over and go to school from her place. I was nervous about it. Who would have thought I'd be nervous about staying with Gram? But I didn't know if I'd feel comfortable in Ralph's house, and even though Ralph had been so nice to me I wasn't sure how comfortable I'd feel spending *hours* with him.

When we got home, Ralph had already started dinner. Before he met Gram, Ralph was the kind of man who sat and read the paper while the women were in the kitchen knocking themselves out. But Gram changed that. She just told him that since they both worked, they were going to share all the household stuff. At first he was shocked, but now he just jumps right in and does what needs to be done. I don't know what he did all the years he lived alone. Gram says he lived on TV dinners and pizza. No wonder he has that little pot belly.

But there he was last night, cutting up vege-tables for a salad, and he looked really pleased with himself. Gram had bought a thick steak to celebrate my first dinner in her home. We don't eat steak at home. Mom says it has too much cholesterol. Why is it that all the best things have too much cholesterol?

Dinner was good, and after a little while I relaxed. When we were finished Ralph stood up and said, "Okay, you women go and spend time alone. I'll clean up."

I was grateful to him, because that was what I wanted. We'd spent the afternoon with Nancy, and had dinner with Ralph, and I wanted my gram to myself. We went upstairs, and Gram took me into the guest room. It was beautiful. Gram had changed it from a study into a warm, comfortable room all in yellow and white. Just like my wedding outfit. I sat on the floor, and Gram sank into a big chair.

"Okay," she said. "How are things going?"

I couldn't lie to her. She wouldn't be Gram if I lied to her. "I miss you. I know I'll get used to it, but I miss you. Sometimes I go up to your apartment and pretend you still live there." Then I added hastily, "I like Ralph. I really do, but I can't help missing you."

Gram smiled. "Well, I should hope you'd miss me for a little while anyway. But no pretending I'm still at home too long. I give you another week and then it's real life, kiddo."

I felt embarrassed, but I had to ask her. "Are you happy?"

"Yes, Lizzie. I am. Ralph is a good man, and I love him."

I was curious. "Like you loved Grandpa? I mean, you married him so you must have loved him, too."

Gram looked thoughtful. "I was crazy about your grandfather. I married him when I was young, and we just were nuts about each other. But, Lizzie, love at my age is different than love as a young woman. It's good and it's lovely, but it's different."

I was glad. I had never known my grandfather, but after all, he *was* my grandfather, and I'd just as soon that Gram didn't feel about Ralph the way she had about Grandpa.

We sat there for almost an hour, and Ralph just left us by ourselves. He *is* a good person. I talked about school. Gram talked about her trip. I talked about what we might do with her apartment. Gram talked about Ralph's family. And then we got to what was really on my mind . . . The Dance.

"I'm scared, Gram. I mean, what if no boy even asks me to dance? And what if I fall all over myself? And what if I spill something on my clothes? And what if my hair looks awful? And why won't Nancy say she'll definitely go? I'd feel better if she did. I don't know why, but I would."

Gram came over and sat on the floor next to me. "Some boy will ask you to dance. I know it. You won't fall all over yourself, either. If you spill something on your clothes, I'll bet you won't be the only kid who does. And your hair will look just fine."

"And Nancy?" I asked.

"I think Nancy is going to wait till the last minute and then decide to go. Leave her be, Lizzie. The more you press her, the more stubborn she will be."

"Tell me about her being stubborn," I said jokingly.

"She's like someone else I know," Gram said, looking right at me.

When I got into bed, I lay in the strange bed in the strange room, and stared up at the ceiling. I hadn't lost my gram, I knew, and I was happy about that, but it felt funny to hear Gram and Ralph laughing in their room. Then he went downstairs to check on all the locks. When he came back up, he stopped at my door. I had left it open. I do that, Diary, in a strange house. It makes me feel less uncomfortable. Well, Ralph leaned against the door and whispered, "Lizzie?"

I sat up in my bed. "Yes?"

"Everything okay?" he asked. "Need anything?"

I smiled in the dark. "I'm fine, Ralph. Thanks."

And you know, Diary, at that very moment I *was* fine. Ralph's house was my gram's house, and I had a place there, too. You know, the way Gram had said loving Ralph was different from loving Grandpa? Well, Gram's living in that house is different from her living here with us, but it's okay.

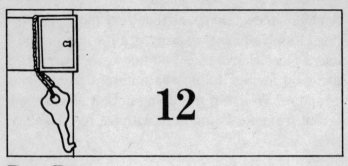

12

Dear **D**iary:

What a day this has been! Tomorrow is The Dance. And that is all anyone in school talked about. Samantha most of all. *She* is even going to a beauty parlor today to have her hair "done." I'm not sure what they are going to do to it, and anyway her hair is so perfect, what could they do?

The decoration committee got all our stuff together to decorate the gym tomorrow. All we have, after all Samantha's suggestions, are balloons. You know what? I have realized that Samantha gives a lot of orders, and has all these great ideas, but she doesn't really want to do any of the work. So someone else just does what he or she wants. That's why we ended up with just balloons in the gym.

The food committee has all the food bought and in the cafeteria refrigerators. All we are having anyway are soft drinks and nibblies, like chips and nuts and stuff. And the music committee got together all the records and tapes they want to play.

So everything seems ready. Except me. I'm never going to be ready.

After school, Nancy and Ericka and I came back here. I dragged some of Dad's crazy food things up to my room, like frozen (only we thawed them, of course) strawberry meatballs, pea-carrot chips, and cheese pretzels (not bad). After we had tried everything, I said to Nancy, "Okay, now say you are going to the dance."

"I don't know, yet," Nancy said, biting into a strawberry meatball. "Yecch."

"Are you referring to the dance or the meatball?" Ericka asked.

"Both," Nancy replied, spitting what was in her mouth into a napkin.

"You're disgusting," I said.

Nancy shrugged. "Who made the law that it was wrong to spit out something that is awful-tasting?"

I changed the subject. "Nancy, you have to come tomorrow. You have to."

"Why?" she asked.

"Because I need you there. I don't want to be there without you."

I could see she was softening. I hadn't thought to try this approach before. Who can resist someone who needs them?

"You'll be fine," Nancy said.

I tried to squeeze a tear out of my eyes, but

just when I wanted to cry most, I couldn't. "I'm scared, too, Nancy. It would make me feel better if I knew at least we could talk about everything after the dance. You could sleep here tomorrow night. You, too, Ericka."

"I have to be home. We're having a birthday dinner for my dad," Ericka said. "But she's right, Nancy. Go to the dance. Then thrash everything over with Lizzie and then, the next day, the three of us will go through the whole thing again."

"Right," I said. "If you don't go to the dance, you'll have to be left out of all the going-over-every-minute stuff."

That got to her. "You mean you and Ericka will talk for days about things that happened, and I won't know what you're talking about? I'll be bored out of my head."

"Right," Ericka and I said together.

"Well . . . ," Nancy said, "I won't dance and I won't talk to anyone, but maybe I'll go and observe."

HURRAH!

The plan for the day is to go to school and then after school go home, change clothes, for those who want to change, which is everyone, and then back to the gym for the dance at four-thirty. I know that lots of times a school dance is right after classes, but we had decided that we wanted time to race home, put on clean clothes, and race back. We will probably all be so out of breath we won't be able to dance.

Dinner tonight was awful. Josh kept asking what boy would ask his (Josh's) little sister to dance. Adam kept saying I didn't know how to dance anyway. My father still wasn't happy about the whole thing, and Darcy thought that dancing with a boy was dumb. I thought families were supposed to be supportive. I read that all the time. Well, my family doesn't seem to know about supporting at all.

Before I went to sleep Mom came into my room. She was pretending to be straightening up, but I knew she had other motives.

"You're going to be fine, Lizzie. You're smart and pretty and Adam has shown you how to dance. What more do you need?"

"A boy to ask me."

Mom sat on the edge of my bed and patted my cheek. "Believe it or not, I know how you feel. I remember my first dance. It was in school, too, and I thought no one would ask me to dance, too. But, you know, much later I realized the boys were just as nervous as I was. Anyway, a few boys danced with me. I wasn't the most popular girl there, but I did all right. And you will, too."

"I hope so, Mom," I answered.

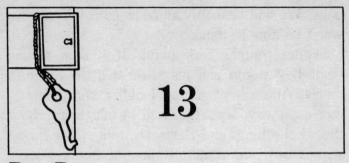

13

Dear **D**iary:

Nancy has finally gone to sleep, and I just couldn't wait until tomorrow to tell you all about tonight. So here I am. Nancy could sleep with floodlights blazing, so my little bed lamp isn't bothering her at all. Just as Gram said, Nancy waited until this morning and then said she'd go to the dance.

It has been the strangest day of my life. Well, maybe not as strange as when Mom brought Baby Rose home from the hospital. I remember that. I don't remember as clearly when Darcy came home.

Anyway, I came home after school and put on my new clothes. Gram was here, and she fixed my hair so that it didn't frizz up too bad. In fact, it looked pretty good. And so did the clothes Gram had picked out. Nancy and I went back to school together. Nancy was actually wearing the clothes Gram had picked out. Nancy and I walked into the gym. It was full of balloons, but hardly looked any different then when we're playing volleyball. And it still smelled like a gym. The food was out on a long table. There was music going, and the boys were all clustered together in one bunch and the girls were all huddled together in another. Great! Nancy and I joined the huddle. Out of the corner of my eyes I could see Billy Watts talking to some of the guys. He looked awfully cute, all freshly showered, his hair still wet, and he had on clean jeans and a clean shirt. I don't mean that Billy doesn't usually look fairly clean, but he *did* look cleaner than usual.

Samantha looked gorgeous. Whatever had been done to her hair made it shine more and curl more. Her black pants were tight and slinky looking. There was no doubt about it, she was the most beautiful girl in the gym. She kept staring over at the boys and smiling. Candace and Jessica were doing the same thing. Then I noticed that Nancy was leaning against the wall. Actually *leaning* against the wall! I grabbed her and whispered, "Didn't you ever hear the expression 'wallflower'? Move away from that wall!"

Nancy shrugged. "Don't get so hysterical. I intend to be a wallflower. That's what I want to be. I told you I was just going to observe."

"You're too much," I hissed at her.

Then some of the boys went over to the food and started munching and drinking, and a few threw some popcorn at each other, but the teachers stopped that fast. And finally, one brave boy went over and asked a girl to dance, and that kind of broke the ice. Soon there were a few couples on the floor and then some more. But I just stood there watching and wishing I was dead. I had been right . . . no one was going to ask me to dance. I thought about going home, but that seemed a worse defeat than just standing on the side, trying to look as if I didn't even want to dance.

But then Robert Wilkins came over and mumbled at me, "Wanna dance?"

I nodded my head and we walked to the middle of the gym, where a number of kids were dancing. Robert wasn't much of a dancer, so I relaxed. After the music stopped, Robert mumbled "Thanks," and I went back to the side of the gym. And then it happened . . . Billy came over and said, "Dance?"

He was actually holding his hand out to me, and I took it. It was a fast dance so I wasn't worried, and we did okay together. Actually Billy wasn't any better than I was. As I was dancing with Billy, I must admit I kind of looked around the gym, hoping everyone noticed I was dancing with cute, cute Billy Watts. Samantha was on the side . . . alone. Imagine that, I was dancing and Samantha wasn't. Then the music stopped, and Billy and I wandered over to the refreshment table. He handed me a Coke, without even asking, and I took it, trying to look casual and at ease. But the kids had filled the cups too full. Now I knew it was going to happen. There was no way I could raise that cup to my lips without spilling the soda all over me. I just stood there, staring at the Coke.

Billy looked at me and then said, "Here, I'll hold it and you just slurp some of it off the top."

He took the soda and I bent over and drank some of it. I made the most awful noises doing it, but I don't see how *anyone* can slurp without sounding gross. I smiled at him gratefully, and he smiled back. We didn't seem to have much to say to each other, but it was okay. I looked over at Samantha again, and she was *still* alone. Only now she seemed to look kind of pale and tense. So the know-it-all cool one wasn't such a big deal after all. So far, not *one* boy had asked her to dance. They looked at her a lot, and they sort of pushed each other in her direction, but no one went over to her. I couldn't figure it out. But I always knew boys were strange.

Nancy was actually talking to Donald Harrington. And she didn't look too miserable. I motioned with my head that she should get out on the dance floor. But she just glared at me and looked away. Okay, so she wasn't dancing. She was at least talking.

The dance was only scheduled for an hour and

a half, and the time almost flew by. I danced with a couple of boys. I wasn't the belle of the ball, but I wasn't an embarrassment to myself, either. Billy danced with me two more times, and by the third time we could even talk to each other. But every time I looked at Samantha she was alone. I still couldn't figure it out. She was so pretty and so cool, and she was even twelve. So what was wrong?

Nancy and I went to the girls' room at one point, because I was sure my hair was frizzing, and I wanted to comb it. On the way, I said to Nancy, "What's with Samantha? She hasn't danced once."

You know, Diary, I don't think I ever realized how smart Nancy is. But she said, "I know what it is. At least, I think I do. She scares the boys. Just like she scares us. She's too pretty . . . too cool . . . too old."

Maybe Nancy was right. "You really are a genius."

Nancy smiled. "Yeah, even if I don't read so well."

We went into the girls' room, and we heard it as soon as we got in there. Someone was crying. Loud. We just stood there, and then a stall door opened and Samantha came out, all red-faced and blotchy. When she saw us she blushed. You could see it through the blotches.

"If you tell anyone about this," she said, "I'll

. . . I'll . . . I'll get even with you somehow."

"We won't tell anyone," Nancy said softly.

I just stared at Nancy. I intended to tell anyone who would listen.

"I'll never get over this," Samantha mumbled. Then she ran out of the room.

Nancy and I just stared at each other.

Nancy and I had to eat dinner with my family and talk a little about the dance before we got up to my room and could *really* talk.

"Well," I said, "what do you think?"

Nancy grinned. "Billy Watts likes you. I know it."

"Do you really think so?"

"Of course," she said. "It's obvious."

"He's kind of nice," I said. "I mean, he isn't too scary or anything. And what about you? You talked to Donald."

"Yeah. He's okay."

"Why didn't you dance, Nancy? You should have."

Nancy glared the Nancy glare. "I told you I wasn't going to." She hesitated. "Maybe next time."

Nancy lay on her bed and looked up at the ceiling. "You know, I felt sorry for Samantha. I mean, she just stood there all that time by herself. Her best friends were dancing, and she was all alone."

"I can't really figure it out, Nancy. Do you really think that the boys are afraid of Samantha?"

Nancy shrugged. "I think so. I mean, look at her . . . with her perfect clothes and her long blonde hair and her makeup."

"She looks pretty good to me," I said. "If I were a boy I'd be very attracted to her. She's the kind of girl, if you're a boy, and you're dancing with her, well, other boys envy you."

Nancy thought. "Yeah, but she makes you feel so . . . so fidgety. Like you're not good enough. Who wants to feel like that?"

"Yeah, and she knows so much about dancing and parties and stuff. Much more than any boy we know."

"I think that's why they didn't dance with her," Nancy said. "She's sort of like a goddess on a pedestal. And who feels comfortable with people on pedestals? And she's old, too," Nancy added. "I mean, twelve is a lot older than eleven. I don't know why, but it is."

"Does that mean we should be happy we're just ordinary?" I asked. "Does that mean if you want a boy to like you, you can't be special? I can't believe that. And I *want* to be special, boys or no boys."

Nancy smiled. "You are special, Lizzie, and Billy likes you. So don't worry."

I was feeling confused. "I guess I just don't

understand boys. I mean, you'd think they would want a girl like Samantha. I'm so intrigued by her, why aren't they?"

Nancy looked confused, too. "I don't know, Lizzie. She just puts them off. But it makes me feel sorry for her. She wants boys to like her so much. It's like her main interest. It would be as if all the birds flew away as soon as I walked into the preserve, and I couldn't watch them at all."

I couldn't quite compare birds to boys, but I sighed and thought about Samantha again. "I guess you're a much bigger person than I am. But I don't feel sorry for her at all. She got what she deserved."

Nancy sat up and looked at me. "Suppose it had been you . . . hardly anyone talking to you all that time. How would you have felt?"

I laughed. "Awful, but I still don't feel sorry for Samantha. Does that make me a creep?" I asked. I was worried.

"No," Nancy said. "Not a creep. Does feeling sorry for her make me a nerd? After all, Samantha has treated me terribly."

"You are not a nerd, Nancy. You are just noble."

We talked a little more, and then Nancy fell asleep and here I am.

Well, Diary, I guess I thought I'd feel like a different person after the dance. And you know,

I don't. I'm still Lizzie Miletti. I'm just Lizzie Miletti who has danced with a couple of boys. Lizzie Miletti who didn't fall down, didn't spill anything on herself, and didn't say anything too stupid. Not too bad. I just wish I were a kinder person and felt something for Samantha. Maybe if no one dances with her at the *next* dance, I'll feel sorry for her then.

Goodnight, Diary. You are a good friend. And I guess you know more about me than anyone else in the world. Tomorrow Nancy and I will go over everything with Ericka, and I'll go over to Gram's and tell her all about the dance. You know, I get scared sometimes, and I worry about a lot of things, and growing up seems so mysterious, but life is pretty good for this eleven-year-old Lizzie Miletti.